Her heart went with him

Waiting for the boarding call, Kyle was quiet. He held Margie's hand in the eerie silence of the tiny airport. The eastern sky was orange; the day was calm without a breath of wind. Birds sang songs of spring outside, in a greening world. And Margie thought, *This is the day he's leaving me.*

"Margie," he said, as if reading the thoughts behind the sadness in her face. "I'll come back to you. I love you."

His goodbye kiss was gentle. He held her tightly against his body, their hearts beating together, and in those moments, the fear lessened for her. But when he pulled away, it returned at once and remained as she watched him walk out onto the tarmac.

He turned, and there was a strange sorrow in his smile. Margie couldn't help but wonder if Kyle, too, felt that things were never going to be the same once he got on that plane....

Regan Forest grew up in the Nebraska sandhills, the setting for *When Tomorrow Comes*. Living close to the land as she did, Regan discovered the power of the Earth to renew itself, a lesson in healing that applies to people, as well. In this touching romance, Kyle and Margie learn that yesterday's sorrow can become tomorrow's joy, just as winter turns to spring. Regan herself now thrives amid the splendor of the Arizona desert.

Books by Regan Forest

HARLEQUIN TEMPTATION
80–THE ANSWERING TIDE
95–STAR-CROSSED
123–DESERT RAIN
152–WHEREVER LOVE LEADS
176–A WANTED MAN

HARLEQUIN INTRIGUE
24–ONE STEP AHEAD
48–HEART OF THE WOLF
84–A WALKING SHADOW

Don't miss any of our special offers. Write to us at the following address for information on our newest releases.

Harlequin Reader Service
901 Fuhrmann Blvd., P.O. Box 1397, Buffalo, NY 14240
Canadian address: P.O. Box 603,
Fort Erie, Ont. L2A 5X3

When Tomorrow Comes

REGAN FOREST

Harlequin Books

TORONTO • NEW YORK • LONDON
AMSTERDAM • PARIS • SYDNEY • HAMBURG
STOCKHOLM • ATHENS • TOKYO • MILAN

To Jim Waltemath, with special love.
And memories of the ranch and sunny days.

Published August 1988

ISBN 0-373-25316-8

1

HER MEMORY WOULD MOVE over him like a cold shadow at unexpected times, and he would feel imprisoned by the memory. He knew he always would unless he found a way to set himself free.

It wasn't that he loved her. Love had gone a long time ago. Only shadows remained. Shadows of betrayal and uncertainty that swept down to remind him that wherever she was, Claire was still his wife.

It was the second week in March, and cold. Kyle Sanders felt the frosty breeze in his face as he rode over the Nebraska hills. A layer of snow padded the frozen ground so the horse's hooves made no sound in the still, icy air.

He followed a barbed wire fence to a corner, stopped and unfolded a tract map from his pocket. Steam of his breath rolled off the white paper. This fence marked the edge of his property line, as he'd thought.

Turning the reins, he headed southeast, following another fence that curved down toward the wide irrigation ditch. Over a hill rise, he found himself looking out on a small meadow. Here the jagged shapes of machinery lay under a blanket of snow like old carcasses.

Kyle rode in closer. The lumps in the snow hid mounds of discarded equipment, barbed wire bales, household junk; the meadow was used as a dumping ground. Bare brown winter trees, losing their cloaks of snow to the breeze, stood on the edge of the meadow like sentinels guarding remains of cast-off yesterdays.

He checked the map again. The meadow was part of his property, all right, but the realtor had failed to mention that it had been used for dumping. An oversight, probably; all big ranches had their dump sites, so it was possible no one was paying attention to where it was when the ranch was divided into sections for sale.

He leaned forward in the saddle. Gentle, affectionate slaps of his leather glove against the solid muscles of his horse's neck were the only sounds in the winter-silent air as he looked out over the snowy meadow and thought of his life. How like this dump his life was—debris covered with a thin layer on top, just enough to hide the jagged edges and the rust and the dirt.

If he could just keep the debris of his life covered, he would have a fresh start here, in this new place—a new town, a new life. With luck he'd find a way to shed the hurt of the past. With a lot more luck, he'd find Claire.

Trees that surrounded his house were dark, lacy silhouettes against the horizon. The sky had clouded to silver. It looked as though there would be more snow. Vapor from his horse's nostrils filled the air as he headed back, skirting the meadow and following along a small frozen stream. This was excellent land he'd purchased— flat land in the river valley and hill land to the north. A small lake, good irrigation from the county ditch if he wanted to plant any crops; he didn't. Hill pasture if he wanted to graze it; he didn't. He just wanted open space to live in.

Ted Prouty's gray station wagon was parked in the driveway. Ted, wearing a plaid coat, got out of the car when the horse galloped into the yard.

"Hey, Kyle, where you been? Out looking over your land?"

The horseman dismounted. "What brings you out here this afternoon, Ted?"

"Been visiting neighbors. I came to ask you something on behalf of all of them."

Kyle's first reaction was one of dread. A gut reaction, the result of years of being pursued and mistrusted. He held his breath and waited.

The other man lit a cigarette and inhaled deeply, blowing out smoke into the cold air. "Do you ice-skate?"

"Huh?"

"Ice-skate."

He blinked. "Yeah, sure. Why?"

Ted looked sideways as if he were hiding something and then smiled broadly. "There's an ice-skating and sledding party at your neighbor's house tonight. May be the last good sledding of the season."

"Which neighbor?"

"Margie Donovan. It's not really her party, though. She just offers her lake and everybody comes. Have you had a chance to meet Margie yet?"

"No. I assumed she was still out of town."

"She's back and anxious to meet the man who bought this last section of her ranch. Neighbors are mighty important here—" Ted interrupted himself with his own impatience, his eyes sparkling. "How well do you skate?"

Wondering why the subject of ice skating was cause enough for Ted to act so strangely, Kyle merely shrugged and watched him change his balance to his left foot and draw again on his cigarette.

"*How* well?" Ted leaned forward anxiously, his straight, gray-blond hair blowing, his ears red with the cold.

"I grew up on a ranch sixty miles from here, Ted. I ice-skated down the river to school."

Ted's eyes widened. "Ever race?"

"Every day, to school and back."

"Win?"

Kyle laughed, slapping the reins against the sleeve of his leather jacket. "Yeah, I always won. Why?"

"*You always won?* Man! Then you got to race Dick Campbell! Dick is self-proclaimed king of the lake. Challenges everybody and nobody can beat him. But if *you'd* challenge *him!* Oh, boy, would I like to see that!"

"Hang on, there! I haven't skated much the past several years. I don't—"

Ted grabbed his coat sleeve. "You've got to! If you could beat Campbell, you'd be doing the whole valley a favor. We're tired as hell of his boasting. I mean, Kyle, we've been sick to death of it for years now!"

"Dick Campbell? Owner of the Campbell ranch over south?"

"That's the guy. Know him?"

"No."

"His cattle are always loose and roaming Margie's land—and yours. You'll meet him at the party. You'll meet everyone at the party." He rubbed his hands together vigorously for warmth and stomped his feet. "Margie is anxious to see your designs for the new auction barn. As auctioneer she'll probably have final say on what we decide. Have you got a sled?"

"Sure." Kyle watched the other man shiver. "Are you sure you don't want to come inside and get warm? I've got the stove lit."

"Can't. I've got to get back to town. By the way, I checked with the phone company to see what the delay is on your phone. They said it'd be two more days, so I guess you'll have to use your neighbor's phone mean-time."

Ted opened his car door and kicked snow from his shoes before he got in. "Margie has one devil of a good sledding hill, so bring your sled. And your skates! Are you really fast on the blades, Kyle?"

"Yeah, I'm pretty fast."

"Hot damn! You'll challenge Campbell?"

"Hell, why not?"

Ted pounded the steering wheel with his open palm and gave out an excited whoop. "It's gonna be a good party tonight!" And with the vapor of his breath filling the car, Ted closed the door, waved and started the engine.

The tires of the car crunched on the hardened snow. Kyle led his horse, Night Sky, into the barn, thinking back to skating parties of his youth. Thinking back to fun and how long it had been since fun was an actual pursuit, even for an evening. This move to Rosewood was the smartest thing he'd ever done. New environment, new people. He shouldn't have waited so long.

The shadow of his past that followed him everywhere would follow him here, too; there was nothing he could do about that. But now, with the purchase of this land, he'd planted his feet, and firmly. Here he would stay. Those who wished to follow him, uproot him, ruin him, would find him easily enough, but somehow he'd live in peace in spite of what Claire had done to him.

Settle for peace for now, he thought. For now. Yet peace was not the same as freedom, not even close. Tortured by the reality of this—even cold as her trail was— he hadn't given up finding his wife, for only then would he ever be truly free.

A FULL MOON cast its white light across the frozen, snow-dusted lake. Kyle stood at the top of the hill, sled under his arm, watching the people around him. Down below and across the small lake a bonfire burned brightly. Figures moved in its orange light like ghostly shadows. On the lake skaters were beaming flashlights in all directions as they glided. And on a small rise above the shore, the lights of the ranch house glowed.

He had arrived late and hadn't yet found Ted Prouty. Ted could be anywhere; there were many people and it was dark. He had introduced himself to a few of the guests, some of the others he'd already met during the past week while he was getting settled in an office in downtown Rosewood.

The sledding hill looked perfect; the slope was just right, and the lake was directly below. With a good start at the top, it should be possible to slide all the way across on the ice to the opposite shore by the bonfire. Three sledders were lining up their sleds for a race. One of them motioned to him to join in as he climbed over the crest.

He accepted the challenge and got his sled in line. Halfway down the slope, two of the racers collided with each other and crash-piled like a demolition derby team. Kyle was ahead of the third, certain to win the race, when he hit a bump at the edge of the ice. His sled flew one direction and he flew another, rolling in the snow while the victor sailed on.

By the thin light of the moon and darting flashlights, he watched the winner scramble off the sled and hurry back. He sat brushing snow from his hair and his ear-muffs.

A slim female figure clad in jeans and a dark ski jacket and cap stood over him. "Are you all right? You're not hurt, are you?"

"Only my pride when you passed me, watching me do contortions in the snow."

The woman's voice was sweet, lilting, but in the darkness he could barely see her face.

She said, "You must be Kyle Sanders."

"How did you know?"

"People have described you. And you're the only person here I don't know." She waited while he struggled to his feet, then offered, "I'm Margie Donovan. My victory was by default just now. I'd have lost the race if you hadn't fallen off your sled."

Kyle scowled. "I didn't exactly fall off. I got bumped off . . . by a . . . bump." He stood looking down at the woman, wishing he could see her better. *This* was Margie Donovan? He had expected a much older woman, not someone in her twenties.

She was saying, "I'd have come by your place to welcome you, but I've been out of town a few days. Winter auctions. Are you settled in? Is there anything I can help you with?"

Nebraska rural hospitality. Kyle had grown up with it and forgotten it during his years in the city. "Thanks, there is something. My phone isn't in and my dog is at the vet's. I need to check on him."

"Of course you can use my phone. Is it serious?"

Kyle was brushing snow from his jeans. "It wouldn't be for a younger dog. He got torn up in a dogfight in town. I've been through this several times with King."

They were standing on the bank of the lake, she on the ice, he on the snow. She had pulled her sled up behind her so it wouldn't get in the way of the skaters who were gliding back and forth on the lake. Their flashlights beamed back and forth, and shouts of laughter rang out in the crisp night air. Light snow had begun to fall. From across the lake more voices and laughter came from the bonfire.

Some people skating behind her shouted as they went by, "Come on, Margie! Chuck has a box of sparklers left from Fourth of July!"

A short man glided up and took her arm. "Where are your skates, Margie?"

She began introductions hurriedly, or tried to. Kyle knew he wouldn't remember names belonging to faces he could barely see in the dark.

As she was being pulled away, she said to him, "There's plenty of cider and beer at the fire...."

Smiling, he gave a small wave to acknowledge the invitation, then knelt to unwind the rope caught under a blade of his sled. Margie Donovan, surrounded by lively voices, faded and disappeared into the night shadows. Pulling the sled behind him, Kyle started around the edge of the lake in the opposite direction.

He left the sled by a tree not far from the bonfire. A path to the house had been cleared of snow. Kyle followed the path toward the bright lights of a sprawling one-story house built of split-log siding. In front was a large stone chimney and a flagstone terrace. Music became louder as he approached. Human forms moved in the light of the windows. The party had spilled into the house.

There was a fire in the fireplace of an L-shaped, rustic room and more than a dozen people dancing. Kyle was greeted warmly and led toward the dining room table, where buckets were filled with snow and cans of beer. He pulled off his gloves, stuffed them into his coat pocket and accepted a beer.

An intoxicated stranger, in answer to Kyle's request, directed him to a closed door on one side of the living room. "Phone's in the den," the man said with a smile. "Help yourself. Margie won't mind."

Kyle unzipped his parka and looked at his watch. It was early yet, and Dr. Hanson, an elderly bachelor, had insisted he could call anytime.

He closed the door of the den behind him against the noise and music of the party. The sound of television reached him first, followed a split second later by shock. On a leather sofa across the room, in front of the television set, lay an enormous pink-and-white pig!

Kyle stopped dead still, blinking. The pig raised its head curiously, snout in the air, making a strange grunting noise, and rolled from the couch, snout wiggling wildly. It grunted again, louder. Kyle backed against the door as it lunged. The pig seemed bent on attacking him!

The full beer spilled from the can over his sweater and trickled onto the polished wood floor as Kyle plopped against the door under the weight of the pig. The creature began licking at the spilled beer, slurping loudly.

At Kyle's back, someone was trying to force open the door. "Newton!" a woman shouted. "Newton, behave!"

With effort, Kyle was able to move sideways to allow her entry. Margie Donovan burst into the room, breathing hard. "Newton, damn you! You've got the manners of a pig!"

At her urging, the pig backed off, but it kept snorting at Kyle, who stood in silent disbelief.

"I'm terribly sorry!" she apologized. "It's not you he's after, Kyle, it's your beer."

"My beer . . ." he repeated incredulously. "Hell, he can have it!"

"No, he really can't. He's not supposed to have it. He's addicted." She was glaring at the pig. "I'm so embarrassed. I realized after I talked to you just now that you meant you needed to use the phone *tonight*, and then I remembered Newton was in the den and of course you wouldn't know Newton or how he'd react if you happened to have a drink with you. He can't be out . . . at the party, you see, because of this alcohol problem he has and all the booze out there. So he had to stay in here...."

"Watching television."

"Yes. At least it's Saturday. His favorite shows are on Saturday—*Hee Haw* and old reruns of *Green Acres*."

Kyle's gaze came to focus not on the animal or the beady little eyes riveted on his can of beer but on the woman before him who was apologizing for the behavior of an alcoholic pig. He hadn't been able to see it in the dark, but she was beautiful—so beautiful he was caught again off guard. Cheeks flushed with cold . . . shining lips . . . skin so flawless . . . strands of silver-blond hair fringed around her black stocking cap. Her gray-green eyes, embarrassed, wouldn't meet his gaze.

"His favorite shows? *Hee Haw* . . . and *Green* . . . ?" Laughter welling up inside him burst out raucously. In spite of her somber eyes, he couldn't hold it back.

His deep, unrestrained laughter relieved the tension. Margie forced a smile. "Usually Newton's manners are without fault. If you hadn't had the beer, he'd have been civilized."

"Let me try to get this straight," he sputtered, conscious—too conscious—of the spell this woman's beauty could weave over him. "You keep an alcoholic pig in the den watching his favorite shows on television because you don't want him to drink at the party."

Margie smiled. "I should formally introduce you. This is retired Sergeant Pig Newton, formerly of the county sheriff's department. Newton is a trained police pig. And a very competent watch pig."

Kyle's eyes moved to the couch, where the pig lay once again, its small eyes shifting from the television to the humans to the beer can in Kyle's hand. The huge, shapeless form filled the couch and hung over the edges.

"Retired from the sheriff's department? For what? Drinking on the job?"

"Oh, no! Newton was retired because of injuries he received in the line of duty. A gunshot wound in the leg. He needed a good home, and I had plenty of room. He wasn't an alcoholic then. My friends are to blame for that—always giving him drinks because he loves alcohol and they found out he's very silly and funny when he's drunk. Before I ever realized the danger, Newton was addicted. Now I'm trying my best to rehabilitate him."

"And he, uh, stays in the house."

"When the weather's like this he does. He hates cold." Margie looked up at Kyle doubtfully. "I hope you're not prejudiced against pigs."

"On the contrary! When I was a kid the neighbors had a couple pigs who used to follow us kids around. We'd swim in the windmill tanks and take the little pigs in with us. They learned their names and thought they were dogs and did whatever the dogs did. One of them tried to wag his tail so often it actually straightened out."

She laughed. "The tail straightened?"

"I swear."

Margie walked over to the pig and patted his big head, soothing him, while her eyes remained on the man. "I thought you were from the city—from Omaha."

"I've worked in Omaha for about twelve years, but in my business I spent so much time traveling around the rural areas I decided to move. Anyhow, I never adjusted to life in the city. I'm a country kid."

"Everyone who has ever seen your work is amazed, including me. One of our local contractors tried to draw plans for the sales barn, but he'd never done one before and we weren't happy with what he came up with. I had seen the barn that you designed in Buffalo County and I was impressed."

He noticed when she smiled that her teeth were alabaster white behind a shine of pale lipstick. His eyes focused with fascination on the most sensual lips he'd ever seen. There was something about the way she moved her mouth, something about her smile.... He forced his gaze away, not wanting to stare, almost unable to keep from doing so.

Margie was saying, "When we asked you to come here to design our auction barn, we never imagined you'd like Rosewood so much you'd want to live here."

"It wasn't the town as much as finding this land for sale. I'd heard of the Donovan ranch. Ted told me you were breaking it up for sale after your parents died and that a section with a lake was still unsold. When he brought me out here one look told me I'd found exactly what I wanted."

She smiled. "Your timing was just right. Ted recommended I accept your offer over another that was slightly higher because he said you'd be a better neighbor."

"Did he now?"

"He did. And I'm glad."

Kyle cocked his head sideways and adjusted the band of his earmuffs, which he'd pushed up into his thick, tousled hair. Now he allowed his gaze to stay on her face. Melted snow was glistening on the wool of her cap like tiny diamonds. And there were similar little sparkles in her light green eyes.

"You haven't had a chance to make your phone call. I'm sorry. I'll leave you some privacy."

"Privacy isn't required. I just need to find out if my dog is well enough to come home tomorrow. But from the look on Pig Newton's face over there, I think it would be kinder if we took the beer out of here. Pigs can smell alcohol a mile off. That much I know."

"They can smell it even when the can isn't open. No bloodhound can compete with a pig. Most people don't know that." She reached for the can. "You're right, though. We should take it out. I'll hold it for you in the other room."

When he came out of the den a few minutes later, he found Margie in the dining room talking with Ted Prouty.

Ted greeted him just as Kyle had expected: "I was telling Margie I convinced you to take on Dick Campbell's standing challenge for a race on ice skates."

Kyle shrugged. "It's chancy. I haven't been on skates much in the past several years. I haven't seen the champion skate, either."

"You have skates, don't you? You brought them?"

"I threw them in my truck."

Kyle could feel Margie's eyes on him as he leaned his head back, gulping his first swallows of the beer.

She warned, "Dick is pretty fast."

"So am I," he said with a smile, wiping his lips.

"Wha-ho!" Ted howled. "This I wouldn't miss! Even as we speak, Dick is down at the lake spinning circles and showing off. Let's go! I'll give him the news while you get your skates on."

"Don't hurry. I want to warm up first."

"Not too long. It's snowing harder. Pretty soon there'll be too much snow on the ice."

Ted exited like a streak. Margie turned to Kyle. "Did you get good news on the phone? Can your dog come home tomorrow?"

"Yeah. He's okay. Strong as hell, old King." He set down his drink and walked toward the door, zipping up his parka. "How fast can Dick Campbell skate?"

"I think his record is eighty-seven seconds around the lake."

Kyle had no idea how fast that was, since he didn't know the lake. Campbell did know the lake, which was a distinct advantage, especially in the dark. He probably shouldn't have gotten himself into this, he thought. It would be lousy if he lost by six yards or more.

He was sitting on the pier, putting on his skates, when Ted brought Dick Campbell up to meet him. They shook hands.

"Always glad for a challenge," the champion said. Wearing army fatigues, the tall man in his thirties had thin strands of red hair sticking out from under an orange stocking cap.

Kyle shook his hand. "I'm not sure what I'm doing, Dick. What's the distance of this race? Once around the lake?"

"That's the usual. Would you prefer twice around?"

"Once is enough. Give me ten minutes to warm up. I haven't been skating all winter."

"Right. Sure. We'll clear the race path in ten minutes." Dick smiled a broad, confident smile in the yellow light of the bonfire that burned brightly on the shore behind the small white pier.

Kyle shoved himself away from the pier and pulled on his gloves. Snow was falling harder, but the ice was smooth. He felt the strength of his ankles. When he was a kid he'd been grand champion of the river. No one had been able to beat him. The feel of his skates on the ice brought renewed confidence. It wasn't something a person ever forgot.

He made a few trial circles. Suddenly Margie was beside him, keeping pace with him. She said, "On the far east side of the lake, just back of the hill, there is a place where some thick reeds poke through the ice. Don't get on the shore side of Dick over there or you may trip."

He slowed slightly, but she was keeping up. "You're fast, Margie. Have you ever challenged Campbell yourself?"

"I sure have. He beat me. And I'd love to see someone outskate him. We all would. For years we've had to put up with his intolerable arrogance about being undefeated on the ice."

"All I can do is try."

Kyle noticed flashlights were beginning to glow in a circle around the edge of the lake, skaters lining each side of what Dick called "the racing path," a wide area of ice along the shoreline. He turned toward the pier again, then back to her.

"Good luck!" Margie called, blinking falling snowflakes from her eyes.

2

COTTONWOODS EDGING THE LAKE were silhouetted in the white glow of moonlight, their bare, frosted branches sparkling whenever a flashlight beam swished across them. It was not a great distance around the lake, even with the sledding hill jutting out into the middle, making a U-shaped shoreline.

Kyle took his place beside Dick Campbell. Campbell, well over six feet, was the taller man; his legs were longer. At the signal he lunged forward with a great burst of speed.

Never a strong starter, Kyle was nonetheless confident of his endurance as he slid forward along the dimly lit racecourse well behind the champion. He was timing his speed to preserve his strength most efficiently, the way he'd learned to do in his youth. There was a psychological advantage, too, in letting the opponent believe it would be an easy victory.

It was like being home again, reliving the past, feeling the icy wind, the sting of blowing snow on his cheeks and his lips. Strength built in his legs and ankles with every slide. His jeans were ice-cold against his legs. With his lungs beginning to burn with cold, he wondered, *can I still do this?*

Gradually he gained on Dick, closing up the distance between them, until finally, on the far side of the hill, Kyle moved up alongside him. The champion moved over, trying to push his challenger toward the shore.

It might have worked if Margie hadn't warned him about the reeds. His skates brushed against them before he realized he had come upon them, so slim and subtle were their shadows in the moonlight. Realizing Dick was deliberately trying to push him into obstacles that could not only slow him down but cause him to take a bad fall, Kyle slowed to get behind him. Anger served him the added flow of adrenaline Kyle needed to lunge forward then, on Campbell's left side, his skate throwing a small jet of ice against his opponent's leg.

On his reserve of strength, Kyle took the lead. Cheers from the bystanders reached his ears as he glided ahead and held a strong lead around the curve and down the north shore of the lake to the finish line at the pier. He crossed the hand-held rope an easy four yards ahead of the former champion. The crowd was shouting and waving.

Panting heavily, lungs aching from ingesting the frosty night air, Kyle leaned into the pier for support and felt the elation of victory. It had been too long since he'd felt the high of victory—in anything.

Over the shouts, Kyle heard only one sound: Margie Donovan's shriek of delight when his legs hit the string of the finish line. The faces around him fused into one face; her smile was all he saw as Margie rushed toward him and planted an excited kiss on his cheek.

Drinks and praises were pushed upon him, and he accepted both graciously. Perspiring under his coat, he felt the warmth of his own body heat and the warmth of victory and the presence of a beautiful woman. He was trying without success to push down the heat of anger— glowing charcoals of anger—that had been lighted in him during the race.

Ten minutes later found him separating himself from the crowd of newfound friends to seek out the former champion of the lake. He found Campbell in the yard of Margie's house, flinging his ice skates into the open door of his truck.

Kyle came up behind him. "You're not leaving, are you, Dick?"

The tall man turned around swiftly. "Does it concern you whether I'm leaving or not?"

"Yeah. We've got some unfinished business."

Yard lights were bright enough so Kyle could see the darkening of the other man's blue eyes. Campbell pulled off his stocking cap with a jerk. His red hair stood straight up in the center of his head where the cap had been.

"You waiting for me to congratulate you, Sanders?"

"No. I might have expected a handshake from a good sport, but I had to learn the hard way what kind of sport my competition was."

Dick's lower lip came out, almost like that of a pouting child. "Hell, it's only a stupid skating race."

"Exactly. Hardly worth causing a man serious injury."

"I don't know what you're talking about."

"The hell you don't. If those reeds had caught under my blades, going at that speed I'd have been damn near killed. Margie warned me about the reeds, or I wouldn't have known. Are you gonna deny trying to push me in when I was trying to pass you?"

"It wasn't deliberate. We were on a curve. I ain't got that much control."

Kyle smiled without humor. "That, mister, is a lie." He took a step closer. "What *I* don't always have control over is my temper. If your friends hadn't surrounded me at the finish line, I'd have laid you flat out on the ice."

The man tried to step back but was stopped by the door of the truck. He glared. "You're not real smart coming as a stranger to this valley and making an enemy of me."

"I didn't do that, Campbell. You did. Cheating in a race is a small thing I can overlook. But I don't forget it when a man tries to put me in the hospital for a reason as petty as yours. I hope we can be cordial neighbors; just don't cross me again."

"Is that a threat?"

"A promise." Kyle was telling the truth about lacking control over his temper. He was grateful that he had been prevented from lashing out at Campbell immediately after the race. He'd probably have hit him and been sorry for it. Often he was sorry when his hair-trigger temper got the best of him. But being sorry never prevented it from happening again.

It took self-control even now to force himself to turn abruptly away from Campbell's hostile eyes and walk away before the poor loser provoked him any further. The tension was tight in Kyle. He would not have minded the release and challenge of a fight.

SNOW CONTINUED FALLING through the night. Margie woke in darkness to a cold dog's nose in her face and the thumping of a tail against the side of her bed. The black-and-tan shepherd stood in anticipation, watching her squint at the digital numbers of her clock radio.

Pulling the quilt over her shoulders, she muttered, "Six o'clock, Angel? Have a heart! I was up late last night...."

It did no good to plead; she knew it wouldn't. The dog whined until she reluctantly got out of bed and stepped into her slippers. Newton was there to greet her in the kitchen, snorting a soft "Good morning." He pushed ahead of the dog, who was bouncing along happily in front of his mistress.

"You needn't shove Angel, Newton," she yawned while she opened the kitchen door. "You were much more polite before you got to be such a big shot around here."

The chill of the unheated back porch was abrupt but not unexpected. Margie breathed in the icy air deeply; it was fresh and good. Snow had drifted against the door, so she had to push to get it open. When Newton, seeing her struggle, lent his massive weight to the effort, one good shove was all it took. Newton knew about doors.

Angel bounded over the new snow, nipping excitedly while Newton slogged resentfully through it on his short legs like a miniature bulldozer.

Pale light was just beginning to pink the eastern sky, reflecting dimly on a world of pure white. All footprints of last night's party had disappeared beneath a fresh blanket, but last night's memories couldn't be so easily erased from Margie's mind. The images of Kyle Sanders were strong: his surprise turning into laughter when he met Newton in the den; his casual confidence about his skill at skating; his alarm and pleased smile when she'd kissed him excitedly at his moment of victory. Suddenly she wondered whether she should have done that.

Shivering in her flannel pajamas, Margie hurried back to the warmth of her kitchen to make coffee.

It was a big room, like most ranch kitchens, with a fireplace of its own and a brick hearth across one end. The walls were papered with tiny yellow and green and red flowers. When she was young, the kitchen fireplace had always been lit early on icy mornings such as this, but fifteen years ago her parents had installed steam heat in the house. Since then the kitchen fireplace was rarely used.

Filling the coffeepot, Margie felt good. Dick Campbell deserved to be defeated last night because he'd tried to cheat. She'd known he would, and so had Ted Prouty. But he'd gone too far this time and everybody knew it. Without her warning, Kyle would have taken a bad spill.

Gathering up some glasses from the party and loading them into the dishwasher, Margie thought about Kyle. Ted Prouty had held out on her about him. Oh, he'd told her about him all right, when she'd signed the final papers for the sale of the land. He'd said the buyer was the architect they'd hired for the auction barn and that if he was married, no wife had so far materialized. What Ted had failed to mention was that the man possessed good looks so stunning that every female head was turning and every mouth gossiping last night as soon as Kyle Sanders appeared at the party.

They wanted to know who he was. So did she. And information was very sketchy. Kyle had seen the land and bought it in a single day, Ted said; he'd known exactly what he wanted. But he'd volunteered nothing about himself during the transaction. Nor during any conversations at last night's party. Still he was friendly; he fit in easily, like a man who had walked these hills and meadows all his life.

Newton was snorting at the kitchen door, wanting back in. She opened the door, saying to the stiff-haired, round body that brushed past her, "You were rude last night, Newton. How can you expect to make friends when you attack people? How do you expect *me* to make friends when you attack people? Our handsome new neighbor thinks you're a bad-mannered lush."

Little beady eyes stared up at her. Ears twitched.

She shook her head. "No, he *wasn't* laughing at you. He was laughing at your choice of TV shows." Reaching down to pat the broad expanse of back with affection, she muttered, "Believe me, Newton, no one in his right mind would laugh at you."

The weather forecast called for more snow today and Margie knew she ought to get out there and plow her road before it was buried any deeper. From the window, she caught sight of her shepherd, Angel, racing about nipping at the velvety white drifts. Branches of bare trees were bending in an erratic wind that whipped off cloud puffs of fresh snow and sent them flying. Even the yellow of the pale sunrise looked cold, frozen.

But memories of Kyle were so warm. His house was a quarter mile off the county road, so he was no doubt snowed in, too, this morning. Margie glanced impatiently at the growling coffeepot.

ANGEL RAN alongside the tractor, leaping in snowdrifts, while Margie slowly chugged up the road. Cold windsprays of snow singed her face from time to time as the snowplow churned and shifted and piled the snow into a neat, long mound at the side of the road.

Any tracks left by Kyle's four-wheel-drive pickup when he returned home last night were covered now. Margie wheeled the small tractor off the road onto the narrow tree-lined lane that led to Kyle's house. Snow had drifted into the fence posts and brown tree trunks.

When she neared the house she saw him—a dark silhouette against the white. He was in the yard trying to shovel out a trail wide enough to drive through. Hearing the roar of the tractor engine, he stopped and turned. She waved. He waved back and stood leaning on his shovel while he watched her approach.

His backyard was also a driveway. Margie drove the snowplow in circles to clear a wide area. Finally the loud engine ceased and she sat looking down at him, tugging on the sides of her stocking cap.

"I got out early to clear my road this morning and I figured I'd do yours, too, since I know you have to get into town to pick up your dog. The county plow was out before six o'clock, so the roads to town are passable. Can you believe how much snow we got last night?"

Kyle reached out his arms to help her down from the tractor, lifting her at her waist. The gesture surprised and pleased her and made her conscious of how bright red her nose must look in the cold.

He said, "You've just saved me a morning's work."

Her nose wrinkled when she smiled. "Aren't these machines wonderful? This is the first year I've had the plow and it sure does ease the pain of winter."

Kyle patted the snow-packed wheel of the tractor as if he were patting the shoulder of a friend. "I thank you both."

"Did you know your mailbox is down? I noticed when I turned into your road. I don't see how the snow could have done it. . . ."

"I think a car did it, somebody driving away drunk from the party last night. It was down when I came home." Kyle picked up his shovel. "I've got a pot of coffee already made, Margie."

"Coffee sounds wonderful!"

Inside his back door, on the utility porch, they kicked off wet boots before he led her into his kitchen. To Margie the house felt strangely different even though Kyle hadn't been here long enough to make any real changes. There were cans of unopened paint in one corner of the kitchen-dining room and sealed boxes stacked against a wall. The potbellied stove in the center of the room was

lit and breakfast dishes—a cereal bowl and coffee mug—
were still on the table.

She said, "This house needs a lot of work. I hated to
sell it in the condition the last tenants left it, but I figured
whoever bought it would be buying the land, not the
house...."

"You gave the house away. I know it and you know it."

"I suppose so. But it's seventy years old and needs so
much work. I didn't want to worry about the repairs."

Kyle was removing his leather gloves. "It's a good,
solid house. With some imagination and a couple strong
arms, I'll make it suit me just fine."

She looked up at him. "Is it just you, then?"

"Huh?"

"You're not married?"

He blinked and answered softly, "It's just me." He mo-
tioned for her to sit down at the round oak table. "And
King, of course, and a gelding quarter horse named
Night Sky I bought a week ago from Jim Ogden here in
Rosewood."

"You bought Night Sky? I know that horse. He's
beautiful! Did you know he was born on the night of a
solar eclipse?"

Kyle nodded. "Jim insists that's why he's hard to
break."

"Jim's had a hard time selling him because he's un-
cooperative. You must be good with horses if you've
chosen Night Sky."

"I grew up with horses and my dad was a good teacher.
I sensed Sky's problem—he's a loner. When there aren't
other horses around, he's reasonable. He hated the bit
Jim Ogden was using, and so did I. Jim would have had
better luck with no bit at all and a different attitude."

A strange feeling settled over Margie. *Who are you?* she ached to ask. This man, this stranger, had such a natural friendliness about him, such a gentleness about him, that he didn't seem like a stranger at all. And he approached animals with understanding and respect, a quality that endeared him to her immediately.

Yet there was something else about him, something undefinable: a wistful sadness in his eyes. In fractured, off guard seconds, there was a strange and brooding kind of darkness that Margie could feel more than see.

As Kyle unzipped his parka and pulled it off, his guest sat back in mild alarm, for he wore no shirt underneath the heavy coat, not even a T-shirt.

Casually, he checked the fire in the potbellied stove and crossed the room to the far end, where a half-full pot of coffee sat on a coffee maker. His shoulders, still darkened by what was left of a deep summer tan, were broad and heavily muscled, his waist slender above tight, very faded jeans. She watched the muscles move in his shoulders while he poured the coffee.

His turning toward her revealed a very broad chest shadowed in dark hair. Margie tried to focus her gaze on anything else—the wall, the coffeepot—for fear her staring was too obvious.

He set a steaming mug in front of her. "Sorry about my state of undress. I wasn't expecting company. I'll, uh, be right back."

Not giving her time to answer, he turned abruptly and padded barefoot from the room. Moments later he returned wearing white socks and a red T-shirt with NEBRASKA CORNHUSKERS lettered in a circle on the front. He sat down at the table across from her.

"Good coffee," she said with a smile.

"Salt's the secret. I add a pinch of salt."

His eyes met hers and lingered too long, as though he were deep in thought—looking at her but thinking of something far away. Finally, with a blink, he moved his gaze away.

Under the spell of pale blue eyes, Margie's gaze, too, moved away, down to his chest and the tight red T-shirt. "Cornhuskers. You went to Nebraska U.?"

"Yep. A hell of a long time ago."

"I was there for two years, before I—" She hesitated, not wanting to lie to him but so used to guarding the truth that evasion came automatically. "I traveled for a year or so, then came back here and went to auctioneer's school and never went back to Lincoln."

Kyle showed no sign of noticing the change in her voice at the mention of her past. "Ted tells me your job requires a lot of traveling."

"Not a lot. To auctions around this part of the state." She sipped the hot coffee. "It was fun last night—the race, I mean. You beating Dick Campbell at his own game. I'm sure everybody's talking about it today—anyhow, everybody except Dick."

"I'm off to a lousy start making enemies with a neighbor."

"You don't have to be enemies, do you?"

Kyle shrugged. "I let him know I didn't appreciate his attempt to kill me last night."

She cringed. "When I saw the way you looked at him at the end of the race, I was afraid you might, uh, want an encounter with him. Dick's not particularly noted for his sportsmanship, which is why it was such a pleasure to all of us to see him defeated on the ice." She looked up at Kyle over the rim of her cup as she sipped. "He cheats at cards, too."

"Yeah? How do you know that?"

"It's common knowledge."

"I can't visualize myself in a poker game with Dick Campbell, but thanks for the warning, anyway, should the opportunity ever arise. And thanks for last night's warning about the reeds, which saved me from considerable pain, I'm sure. We met only hours ago, and already I owe you a pile of favors."

"Who's tallying? You're the new kid on the block. It all evens out eventually."

The room seemed to be getting darker, although the red wooden shutters at the window were opened wide. She turned toward the weak morning sunlight. "Good Lord! It's starting to snow again!"

He was spooning more sugar into his cup. "It's not the best day for driving. Are you planning to go into town? I can pick up anything you need if it would save you a trip."

"Oh, great, thanks! I can use some milk and bread, but I wasn't planning to brave the snowy roads to pick them up. If it keeps snowing, the roads will get worse...."

"My truck can get through, now that you've cleared my way to the county road." Kyle leaned back and studied her in a spell of silence.

He asked, "The shepherd that came in with you—is it your dog?"

"Yes, that's Angel. She's gone back home, probably following some animal's trail across the meadow. Sometimes she pretends she's a great hunter, but none of the local wild critters are fooled for a minute."

"I'm relieved to hear you say 'she.' My old warrior has a certain code of chivalry. Much as King loves to fight, he won't go to battle with a female. Angel is a handsome lady. King will probably fall in love."

"If he does, you could end up the godfather of some fine German shepherd puppies." Margie tucked her hair loosely into her stocking cap and pulled her jacket from the back of the chair. Her cheeks still hadn't warmed, but her hands were thawed by the hot coffee mug. "I won't hold you up. King must be very anxious to get out of the hospital and come home."

He walked out with her and helped her onto the tractor as though it had never occurred to him she had climbed up and down on it a thousand times before he ever knew her. Everything he did, it seemed to her, was like that: a statement of his masculinity responding to the femininity of her. He saw her as a woman first, a friend second. Standing in his yard watching the tractor chug out and down his narrow road, he waved once, when she turned around. Even with the cold wind whipping snow around her, Margie experienced a deep sensation of warmth.

IN MIDAFTERNOON it was still snowing. A fire blazed brightly in the living room. Newton and Angel were asleep in a far corner, their noses almost touching. At the sound of wheels in the drive, Margie left her desk and the stack of bills and went to the window.

The mail truck pulled up in front. Leaving the motor running, a man got out, huddling against the wind.

She met him at the door. "You didn't need to drive up to the house, Phil. I can get to the mailbox. But as long as you're here, I'll bet you can use some hot coffee."

"I'd love it, Margie, but I'm running three hours late with these blessed roads. I drove in to ask if Kyle Sanders has moved in yet. The mailbox has been knocked down."

"Yes, he's moved in, but he's not there now. I'll give him his mail if you want to leave it here."

The offer was already anticipated; the man had Kyle's mail—a single letter—in his hands, along with hers. He handed the stack to her. "I hear he's drawing up plans for a sales barn. Does this mean we're really gonna get that barn built, Margie?"

"Building will start at the first thaw. This architect Kyle Sanders is a specialist, and he's good. I'm glad we waited." She watched steam form on the man's glasses. "If you can't take time out for a cup of coffee, Phil, then take a thermos of it with you. I have some already made."

"I will, and gratefully, Margie. It's getting colder by the hour. But I'll not step in with these wet boots. Where's Pig Newton? He's usually right here at the door."

"Newton can't take the weather. He's asleep by the fire with one eye open. I'll be just a minute."

She tossed her mail onto a chair as she went by and dropped Kyle's letter on the coffee table, noticing the return address on the envelope. The sender appeared to be an Omaha law firm.

It was nearly four o'clock when Kyle arrived. His pickup roared up, and responding to the sound of an unfamiliar vehicle, both Newton and Angel were standing with her at the door when Margie opened it.

He stood with a paper bag, looking uncertainly from her to the dog to the pig. "There's no booze on me this time, so can I assume it's safe?"

She smiled. "Come in. Where's King?"

"Home sleeping on his rug by the stove. He isn't up to handling the excitement of meeting Newton and Angel after a night in the hospital and a dozen stitches in his face."

Rather than hand it to her, he set the paper bag on the floor while he wriggled out of his cowboy boots. "There was a sale on ice cream, so I got us some. Chocolate. I figured there was no danger of it melting on the way home. And I got marshmallow topping. How's your sweet tooth?"

"Very healthy, thanks. Marshmallow sundaes with chocolate ice cream are my favorite."

"Mine, too. I had a hunch about it. I said to myself, 'Margie Donovan is a sundae kind of woman.'"

She cringed. "I do love sundaes, but I hope you didn't go to all that trouble just so you could hit me with that pun."

"What pun?"

She studied his expression of innocence and couldn't decide on his degree of guilt. "Never mind. You figured this is great weather for ice cream?"

"Why not? Cold is stimulating. A man can drink hot toddies for only so long."

"Do you want some ice cream?"

"Does a bear want honey?"

"I should know better than to ask a man who puts three spoonfuls of sugar in his coffee."

He grinned. "My one and only weakness and you've discovered it already."

She bent to pick up the sack, but he quickly interceded, kicking his boots aside. "I'll get that."

He was doing it again—treating her as if she were a lady wearing silk and lace instead of jeans and an oversize plaid flannel shirt. He was such a strange combination of ruggedness and gentleness—a man who knew how to flatter her without seeming to realize that he was flattering her. A man who liked her strength but treated her as though she were as fragile as a butterfly. Kyle confused her, fascinated her...and wakened new feelings in her.

While she led him through the living room and into the kitchen, he was reaching down with his free hand to pet the animals and whistling the tune "Sunday Kind of Woman."

"*That* pun!" she said accusingly without looking back.

"I'm innocent."

"Of course you are." She turned around. "Make yourself comfortable by the fire, Kyle. I'll fix the sundaes. The mailman left a letter for you here because your mailbox is down. It's there on the coffee table."

He glanced at the envelope as he passed by. An expression of combined shock, dread and curiosity clouded his eyes while he set the grocery sack on the kitchen counter and offered his services in making the sundaes, since they were his idea. Newton was pushing against his leg, taking great interest in what might be in a bag that smelled like supermarket.

"Newton wants your forgiveness for last night," she said as she began to unpack the groceries. "You go on ahead and make peace with him. I can take care of this."

Kyle scratched behind the animal's ear. Friendly, whispered snorts were his reward. Realizing he was doing something right, he led the pig back into the living room, where he picked up the letter before he settled on the rug by the fire with Newton and Angel beside him.

Margie could see him through the arch, petting the animals, talking to them before he leaned back against a chair and opened the letter.

Marshmallow cream was spilling over the side of the dish before she remembered what she was doing, because her full attention was suddenly riveted on Kyle. The expression on his face frightened her. His eyes narrowed, his brow creased and the cords of his neck stiffened visibly with the tightening of his jaw. Whatever that letter contained was, at best, unexpected news.

He ran his fingers nervously through his thick brown hair as he read, then leaned an elbow on his raised knee. His head came to rest in his palm as if he had momentarily lost the strength to hold it up. His face was hidden then, as he kept reading—or staring at—the letter; she was unsure which.

He was frowning when he shifted, folded the paper, returned it to the envelope and looked with some concern at his watch. She wondered why he would look at his watch so frantically.

She couldn't ask, of course. His mail—indeed, his *life*—was none of her business. But it was obvious that something in that letter from a law firm in Omaha had shaken Kyle and shaken him badly.

3

"Nuts?" she called from the kitchen.

Kyle was pulled back from the dark recesses of his private thoughts. "What?"

"Do you want nuts on your sundae?"

"Sure, the works. Throw on anything you want." He folded the envelope and slid it into the pocket of his red-and-black plaid shirt.

When she handed him the dish, he lifted himself from the floor and slid onto the chair. The dog and the pig moved in closer in anticipation, but a word from Margie sent them to the opposite side of the room.

"Don't look at them when you're eating," she said. "They're experts at making you feel guilty."

Kyle turned his concentration to his dish. "What's this on here?"

"Malt balls."

"Right, I knew that. What's a sundae without malt balls?"

Licking marshmallow from his lips, he asked, "How did a retired police pig happen to end up at your house?"

"I'm not entirely sure. Heaven knows, I never planned it. Actually, Newton has his own quarters in the barn, but in this weather he gets cold and lonesome out there, and I haven't the heart to shut him out. Honestly, Kyle, I had no idea how bright pigs were until I met Newton."

"How *did* you meet Newton?"

"A friend, a sheriff's deputy, brought him here one day and asked if he could stay. Newton had been shot in a robbery attempt and couldn't work anymore, and you know what happens to pigs without jobs. My friend couldn't bear such a fate befalling Newton. They were comrades, after all. I said Newton could stay until he found some other place, but of course he never did, and anyway it didn't take long for Angel and me to become attached to him. I've never had a more fascinating friend."

Kyle was looking at the fire and not at her when he answered, "I don't think *I've* ever had a more fascinating friend than the lady I'm sitting next to right now."

Margie licked ice cream on her spoon. "You mean because I have a pig in my house?"

"That...among other reasons. You're a lady who lives life the way she wants without worrying about what other people think. I admire that, Margie. I find it refreshing."

She looked surprised. "Is that how you see me?"

"It's how you are."

"Is it?"

He stretched his legs and waited for her to say more. When she didn't he asked, "Isn't it?"

Her eyes clouded. "I haven't thought about it ... for a long time...."

She seemed suddenly to have moved a long way away. His curiosity rose. "Haven't thought about what, Margie?"

Jolted gently back to the present, she hesitated. "Oh, about being concerned over what people think. I...used to be. You know how it is, growing up in a small valley."

"Yeah, I do know. And I know most people never change as long as their surroundings never change.

That's how valleys like this stay the same, generation after generation. I'll bet some of the gossip around here is twenty years old."

She smiled. "Yes."

"It was like that where I grew up, too. Something must have happened to cause you to change."

Margie shrugged, but she knew she was unable to hide her discomfort at his question. Perhaps she hadn't changed that much, she thought, because she still guarded her secrets with a kind of quiet vengeance. To live here, she had to.

She tried to will away the dull pain of memory by ignoring his question. "I have the distinct impression that you, too, live your life as you want, with little concern about impressing people."

His pause conveyed to her that he had noted her evasion of his question. Attempting to answer hers, he began, "I try to live my own life. It's harder when . . ." But his voice trailed away, until the only sound in the room was the popping and crackling of the fire.

"When what?" she prodded after a long silence.

"Uh . . . nothing. I'm just . . . rambling. . . ."

Conversation edging at their past lives was awkwardly going nowhere. Margie eyed him curiously. He was intent on eating, or so he would have her believe. *This man has secrets, too,* she thought. All the signs were there; she knew them well. And she pulled back from questions that would have ordinarily been natural. "I think you'll like Rosewood—this valley. Are you going to work out of your home?"

"No, that's too difficult when I live in the country. I've leased an office in town, over the bank, but I haven't moved into it yet." He chewed, crunching loudly. "Hey, these malt balls are all right!"

It was impossible for her to forget the letter that had stunned him so; she couldn't help wondering why his first reaction had been to look at his watch. The longer she thought about it, the more her curiosity goaded her.

"You'll have to get creative about fixing your mailbox because the post is broken in half and the ground is frozen."

"Yeah. I'll think of something, even if it's temporary." He looked at the gray-white sky outside the window. "I'd better get to work on it before it gets dark, though I'll be honest, Margie, it isn't easy forcing myself away from your warm fire—and your company."

"The fire is always here."

He scraped up the last bite of ice cream and set the dish down. "Thanks for the sundae."

"Thank *you* for the sundae. I'd have offered you something hot and boring, like coffee and vanilla wafers. I appreciate you picking up the groceries."

"Anytime." He stretched luxuriously and rose. "You're right, Margie. I like Rosewood. I like it better every day."

DRIVING THE MILE of white road between her house and his, Kyle caught himself through habit looking in the rearview mirror.

"Idiot!" he muttered aloud. "Even Brockmeier isn't crazy enough to be out in weather like this!"

Wayne Brockmeier, in his relentless pursuit, probably already had his new address. Kyle knew Brockmeier could show up in Rosewood any day. But not likely this day, in the snow.

Kyle had forgotten what it was like to live without being constantly followed, constantly spied on. It wasn't something a man could get used to. *Damn!* he thought. Wayne Brockmeier was so persistent, he'd be bothering

Margie the way he had infringed on the lives of everybody Kyle knew or had ever known. If he and Margie were to get very friendly, she was sure to be harassed. Kyle ground his teeth in anger. He wouldn't stand for it, he decided. He had put up with a hell of a lot from Brockmeier's insurance company, but there was a limit to what he could take. Brockmeier had better not push him any farther, because he didn't intend to take it. They'd better stay the hell out of his personal life in Rosewood!

Why, all of a sudden, did it matter so much more? Kyle had no sooner asked himself the question than he knew the answer: Margie Donovan. She was the first breath of fresh air in his life in more years than he wanted to remember. Margie made him think of springtime and summer flowers and the feeling of sun on his skin. She made him remember good things, sweet things, soft things. It had been so long since he'd remembered, so damned long!

Adjusting the rearview mirror assured him that there was nothing behind him in the dreary twilight but a snowy, deserted road. For the moment nothing was following him except the ever-present shadows. And unanswered questions from the past. And uncertain predictions of the future.

His big German shepherd, King, met him with wild enthusiasm at the door. There was a chill in the house. With the dog hanging at his heels like a puppy, Kyle brought in logs from the back porch to build a fire. There wasn't much light left of the day. To hell with the mailbox; it was too late to work on it now. The day was shot. He fed the dog and made himself a pot of strong coffee before he sat down on the couch with his sketch pad and a collection of diagrams and specifics he'd made for the

McKinsie ranch—the largest private working barn he'd ever been commissioned to design.

But concentration came hard. Instead, he took out the letter from Horace Young, his lawyer in Omaha, and re-read it.

Dear Kyle:

My sources tell me there are rumors circulating around Miami, Florida, that someone in that city has seen Claire in the past few weeks. I'd like your permission to rehire John Dillon or someone else from Dillon's detective agency to follow up on this.

Please don't make any attempt to go to Miami or search on your own because as long as you're suspected of conspiracy you can't risk how it would look if you should happen to find Claire yourself.

Just be careful and let me, as your attorney, make the moves. I doubt there's anything to these rumors, but if Claire is in Miami, Dillon's agency can probably find her.

Sit tight.

Horace

Kyle crumpled the letter in his fist, grimacing. The initial relief that there was at last some sort of lead was overridden by a wave of anger. Why would Claire have put him through this?

He felt—had always felt—she was alive. It puzzled him that no one had been able to find her. The insurance company had certainly tried. And he'd tried.

King rested his big head on his master's lap, sighing contentedly. Kyle petted him while he sat staring into blue and yellow sparks of the fire, feeling flames of bitter memories singeing his consciousness. Familiar, clinging memories of flights above mountains, time and time again.

His bitterness was cold, unforgiving, when he thought of Claire alive. But she may not be alive; he had to face that, too, and he didn't want to. Tomorrow he'd get to a phone and call Horace Young in Omaha and find out more about the vague "rumors" in Miami. It had been too late today to phone, from Margie's.

Margie...

He had to keep Brockmeier away from Margie, no matter what. He wouldn't have her dragged into anything so damned dirty, just by association with him. What was worse, Margie assumed he was single, and he wasn't about to tell her otherwise, because that was just as much a lie.

A man couldn't escape by changing towns. There were no new beginnings. There were no endings. There were just years tumbling over years. And when seven years had gone, what then? Would Brockmeier get off his back? Would Claire return? If she didn't, would he be charged with her murder? Or would he be cleared of the mountain of suspicion against him through lack of evidence? Would Margie still look at him the questioning way she did today, with eyes that spoke acceptance?

Kyle sighed shakily, drained his second cup of coffee, leaned back and closed his eyes.

MARGIE WOKE to the wailing sound of wind and the slashing of wind-whipped snow against the windows. It was barely light. The dog, still sleeping on the floor beside her bed, raised her head slowly and looked at her mistress as if to say, "It's too early to get up."

"It sounds bad out there," Margie said aloud as she rose and crossed the room to open the curtains. Gray-white light filtered in, mingling easily with the shadows. Swirls of snow scraped the glass. Beyond the house, where the first sun usually shone on the shingled roof of the barn and the corrals, she could barely make out the outline of the buildings through a howling white glaze.

"It's a blizzard!" she said, and the dog looked up at her with a yes-I-know-I-can-hear-it expression.

Seconds later she heard Pig Newton snorting loudly, a peculiar alarm snort that roused the dog to excitement. Angel jumped up with a sharp bark and ran out of the room. The doorbell sounded.

Trouble, Margie thought instinctively. No one made social calls at sunrise in a blizzard. Hurriedly, she stepped into her jeans and pulled on a heavy sweater, pushing her uncombed hair away from her eyes. It wouldn't do to keep anyone standing outside.

With bare feet and strands of loose hair falling about her face, she opened the door. Dick Campbell stood there in the shelter of the front porch. Behind him, tied to the porch post, was his horse. As she opened the door, a gust of snowy wind blew in. Dick stepped inside quickly, brushing snow from his eyes.

"Good heavens, what's wrong?" she asked, urging him further into the warmth.

His lips were stiff from the cold. Even his voice seemed half-frozen. "I didn't hear any forecast of this blizzard. I've got thirty head of cattle in my hill pasture, including a champion bull! I need some help getting them rounded up and down to shelter. I need all the riders I can get!"

She glanced outside the window, then back at him. "Which pasture?"

"The one directly north of my house." Campbell rubbed his hands together but didn't take off his gloves.

"I rode over to Skully's, and Bill and Luke are saddled up and on their way to the pasture."

"Okay, I'll get there as soon as I can. I'll stop and get Kyle Sanders. We'll find you up there."

Campbell squinted. "Does Sanders know anything about rounding up cattle?"

"He says he grew up in a saddle. And he's got one hell of a quarter horse. He bought Jim Ogden's Night Sky."

Campbell paused less than a second while Margie tried to interpret the strange look that entered his eyes. "We need him, then. Get his help if you can." He turned toward the door. "I've got a dozen Brahmas in that herd."

"Damn," she said, remembering her misgivings about Campbell keeping the Indian cattle. "We'll get them down if it's humanly possible, Dick."

He nodded gratefully and let himself back out into the cold. Margie held the door open so Angel could dash outside.

She rushed to the bedroom for heavy socks and another sweater and to the kitchen for her snow boots. In her haste, it took some time for her to notice Newton standing by the kitchen door looking pathetic.

She couldn't help but smile. "Well, hurry, then, make it fast, Newton. I have to get going."

She let the pig out, grabbed a handful of granola cereal from the box and washed it down with a few swallows of milk. This nourishment was going to have to fuel her energy through some grueling hard work.

Newton didn't stay outside long. He soon was curling down contentedly on his favorite rug in the living room, while Margie wrapped up in her warmest coat and hat and scarf and headed out toward the barn with Angel at her heels.

The wind was at her back as she rode the mile to Kyle's house. This helped. The snow was blowing so hard that the hoof prints of Dick Campbell's horse were already impossible to follow. Branches of bare trees bent over her as she rode down the lane in a world of silence save for the moans of the blustering wind. She pulled her wool scarf up over her face. Under the scarf, her breath felt warm and moist.

A light was shining from Kyle's barn. Riding up to the door, she dismounted, opened it and led her horse inside behind her. Angel followed close behind. Kyle was hammering boards over a broken window. At the sound of the wind rushing in, he turned. King dashed toward them, tail wagging wildly. Angel stood still, showing cool interest.

"I'm glad you're up and out already," Margie said. "Dick Campbell has some stock stranded in the hills and needs help getting them down to shelter."

With no sign of hesitation Kyle finished pounding in the nail, hurriedly drove in another, then set the hammer down.

"Okay," was all he said as he pulled a saddle down from a post. "Do you know exactly where?"

"Yes. Straight north of his house, just over the ditch. Which makes it almost due north on the compass. I brought a compass. The pasture is large, but the cattle will all be huddled together. All we have to do is find them. There are some riders already on their way. Dick says there are a few purebred Brahmas in the bunch."

"Yeah? Those Brahmas will be the problem," Kyle said, grunting as he tightened the cinch. "Campbell really asks for trouble keeping Brahmas in winter pastures."

Except for some resident cats, Night Sky was the only animal in the big old barn and he roamed it freely. He'd settled himself into a stall filled with fresh hay, which smelled warm and clean. Now he gave a small whinny as Kyle led him toward the main door, which was banging in the wind. The dogs were following behind, sensing excitement.

Margie said, "You'd better get on another layer of clothes. The chill factor is fierce."

"Yeah, you're right." He handed her his horse's reins and hurried out toward the house.

She led the horses into the yard, fastened the door securely behind them and met Kyle in the yard outside the front porch. He said nothing as he mounted. The wind and blowing snow made conversation difficult if not impossible as they rode at a reasonable pace, mindful of conserving the strength of their horses. The shepherds followed, bounding along in the snowdrifts like two excited children.

The task before them took a good part of the morning. While the Hereford cattle huddled with their backs to the wind, it was necessary to herd them south, against the slashing snow blowing from west and north. The drifts were getting so deep the animals could make only slow progress. Margie and the dogs and two men herded the Herefords down, while Kyle and Dick and two more men took on the challenge of the Brahmas. Unused to the cold and therefore lacking the instincts to survive it, the Brahmas did not protect themselves well. When their eyes froze shut, they panicked. They couldn't withstand this kind of weather; efforts to save them might be useless.

Helping urge the white-faced cattle along over the snowdrifts, Margie caught sight of Kyle and another rider as they struggled to bring a Brahma to the moving herd. She could identify Kyle's silhouette by the way he moved on the horse and by the broadness of his shoulders. She could hear echoes of his shouts mingled with the others.

The group of experienced cowboys worked efficiently and quickly to get the job done. Within three hours all the cattle, including the Brahmas, had been brought down to shelter.

At the Campbell ranch house, Dick's wife, Sharon, a plain, shy woman who seldom said much to anyone, invited them inside for coffee and food. Margie politely refused, saying she didn't want to get warm and then cold again riding the two miles home. Kyle, thanking her, insisted he, too, wanted to get back home before the drifts got any deeper. The storm was still blowing fiercely. It was not yet noon.

When they reached the cutoff to his house, a road now buried in snow, Margie offered, "If you want to come back with me I'll fix you an enormous breakfast."

"That's an offer I can't refuse. There's nothing like riding all morning in a blizzard to stimulate a man's appetite for a hot breakfast." Because of the wind, they had to shout to hear each other.

"Sharon Campbell had food there."

"Not the same." His voice came back on a whine of wind.

The riders leaned forward into the wind, shielding their eyes as they turned north. The world around them was white and silver, snow and wind. The weary horses picked up their pace, knowing they were heading in the direction of home and shelter. The dogs, tired, cold comrades by now, lagged some distance behind.

Kyle had offered to take care of the horses while she started breakfast, so she went on into the house ahead of him. Her body tingled in the warmth, a tingle bordering on pain; she hadn't realized how cold she was. Her face was stiff from the chill. After changing clothes, she got busy in the kitchen.

Breakfast was underway by the time Kyle appeared at the back door with an armload of firewood. Margie heard the howl of wind as the door opened. Newton was at the back entrance at once, almost tripping him, while he set the wood down and began to pull off his soaked boots. The dogs rushed in. King stopped in surprise when he encountered Newton, looking at the pig and back at Kyle as if demanding some kind of explanation. His master's laughter seemed assurance enough that the ungainly pink creature did indeed have permission to be here.

"The dogs are wet," he called to Margie.

"It's okay. They can get dry by the fire, but what about you? You have no dry clothes. I threw a wool blanket on the couch if you want to strip down and wrap up in it."

"I don't suppose it's too easy building a fire while wrapped up in a toga, so I'll do that first. Do you ever use this kitchen fireplace?"

"Rarely, but let's use it today and make two fires. I feel as if my feet will never thaw."

From the stove, frying bacon, she watched him build the fire from the logs and kindling she kept on the back porch. His jeans hugged his hips tightly as he bent at the hearth. Loose strands of his heavy, dark hair that hadn't been protected by his ski cap were damp and shining. He had hung his damp parka on a hook on the back porch. At least this time, she thought, he was wearing something under his coat, a navy-blue sweater over a flannel shirt.

"The coffee's ready," she offered.

"It smells fantastic in here. Pig Newton doesn't mind the smell of bacon?"

"He's never voiced a complaint." Margie poured out two large mugs of coffee and remembered the three spoonfuls of sugar for his. "Do you like cheese omelets?"

"Do anteaters like ants?" He accepted the mug gratefully and set it on the stone hearth while he lit the fire. It took quickly, filling the room with soft orange light.

"You make a fine fire, sir."

"And you, ma'am, make a fine cup of coffee." He sipped and stood back from the fire, then looked down at his pant legs. "I'm pretty wet. Guess I'd better hang my jeans in front of the fire." When he left the kitchen, Newton was beside him, following like a clumsy puppy.

Moments later he returned with the blanket wrapped around his waist. He drew a chair near the fire and hung his jeans over the back.

Margie had everything on the table—butter, honey, orange juice, the coffeepot. She brought a basket of warm biscuits and handed him his plate. The omelet was fluffy and fat and steaming hot. Kyle groaned in anticipation.

"What a winning combination! My appetite and your cooking!"

He ate without pause for a full minute, then looked up from his plate. "Margie, your sweater and your cheeks are the same color."

"The color of frostbite?"

"No, the color of pale pink rose petals. Such a soft color. Suits you perfectly."

"I'm soft? You didn't think I was soft up there on the hill this morning, did you?"

He gazed at her strangely. "We're not talking about the same kind of soft." A small silence fell while he took another bite of his omelet and washed it down with juice. "I meant—" He cleared his throat. "Well, I can't say from firsthand knowledge, but my educated guess is that you're softer than anything I've touched in one hell of a long time."

Margie flushed and pushed the bowl of honey toward him when he reached for a second biscuit. "I noticed," she began, feeling the need to change the subject, "you didn't hesitate when I told you it was Dick Campbell who needed help this morning. I wasn't real sure how you'd react, since you were pretty angry at him over trying to push you into the reeds."

"Hell, this was an emergency. The cattle were the ones in trouble. I'm surprised anybody around here still owns Brahmas after what happened in 1949."

"You know about the blizzard of '49?"

"Everybody in this part of the state who is old enough to remember is still talking about it, including my father. Drifts as high as the barn and most of the Brahma cattle lost."

Margie looked up at the branches bending in howling wind outside the window. "This storm isn't that bad, but it's bad enough."

"If it keeps up, I'm not going to be able to persuade Night Sky to try to make it home. He's as cozy in your barn as I am in here."

"If it keeps up, you may not be able to get home. I didn't think of that when I asked you to breakfast."

"Neither did I, but if I had, I'd have come anyhow." He looked at the clock on the wall. "It's after noon."

"Yes."

He spooned honey onto his biscuit.

"I listened to the radio for a few minutes while you were in the barn," she said. "There's not much happening in town today. Schools are closed and most of the businesses. The county isn't even attempting to do anything about the roads until it stops snowing."

"And as for me," he said, "there's no place I'd rather be than by your fire."

It was difficult to see the coming of evening because the sky was dark and the wind still blew. Minutes had tumbled into hours. He had helped her with the dishes, and they had moved into the living room. They sat on the floor, all five of them. The dogs and the pig settled down to sleep with their noses almost touching.

The fire crackled and spit and made shadows on the wall. Margie leaned back against the couch, holding a glass of hot apple cider, and sighed. "I can't remember when I last spent an afternoon doing absolutely nothing."

Kyle stretched his legs in front of him, wriggled his bare toes and yawned. "What do you mean, nothing? We've been busy all afternoon."

She smiled. "Once or twice you nearly nodded off."

"Nah. I was just listening to your music. Warm fires and music make me drowsy."

Setting her glass on the floor, Margie began to hum to the soft strains of music from her stereo. "You don't talk much about yourself, Kyle. I mean, other than your work."

He rubbed his neck. "Neither do you, I've noticed."

"Me?"

"Yeah, you."

"What's to talk about? You can see how simply I live. I have my work and my home and my friends. I'm a very ordinary woman."

"I disagree. There's not a thing ordinary about you." Kyle picked up a small white marble statue from the end table and gazed at it for a time in silence. "Romulus and Remus suckling the wolf. I saw statues like this in Rome."

She watched the way his fingers moved over the smooth marble. Sensuously. "You're the first person who has seen that statue here who knew what it was."

"I don't suppose too many of your neighbors have been in Rome," he said.

"No."

"But you have."

She paused. "And you have."

"Yeah."

Her smile came softly. For a time both watched the fire, Margie hugging her knees, Kyle touching the statue. Eventually he set it down and said, "Vacation?"

"What?"

"Europe."

"Oh . . . yes. It was . . . a long time ago." Her eyes reflected the firelight. "You, too? Vacation?"

"I took a side trip to Rome the summer I spent in Europe. I was studying architecture in Holland."

"Oh? Windmills?"

He laughed. "Barns. I was all over Europe looking at barns. I can drive through the U.S. today and tell you the nationality of the original immigrants on any farm just by the designs of the barns they built."

"I like barns," she mused.

"So do I."

Her shoulders rose in a sigh. "You know, that's all I've learned about you—that you like barns. That and the fact that you can skate faster than anybody I ever met."

"It's more than most people know about me."

She looked at him quizzically, believing him. "Why?"

"I get bored talking about myself."

"You deliberately avoid the subject of yourself or your life before you came here."

He shrugged as if he didn't know what she was talking about, but he did.

"You do it very well—avoid talking about yourself. Like it's a practiced art." Her voice was light, slightly teasing.

"You should know."

"What does that mean?"

"I don't know," he said honestly. "You're very astute, Margie, and you're more than a little mysterious yourself sometimes, whether you like to think so or not. What is it you want to know about me?"

"I wonder why a guy like you is single. I wonder if you've ever been married."

4

IT WAS THE QUESTION Kyle dreaded most. He'd expected it sometime, knowing he'd have to answer when she asked. Yes, he'd been married. He was married now. Or maybe he wasn't; he had no way of knowing. For a moment he merely looked at her, then looked away.

Margie sensed something wrong. The expression in his eyes told her he would much prefer to avoid that simple question, and there could be only one reason for his not wanting to answer. A stir of dread mixed with disappointment moved within her.

At length, he answered awkwardly, "Yeah...I have...."

"Why do you hesitate, Kyle? Are you still married?"

His gaze shifted like that of a child who is confronted with a matter he wishes to avoid, usually because of guilt. For a time Margie thought he wasn't going to answer at all, but finally he muttered, "Separated," from the side of his mouth.

Something definitely wasn't right. Usually so casual about everything, Kyle had suddenly withdrawn and pulled back into himself, all but taking his answer with him. He couldn't have made it plainer that he didn't want to talk about his marriage.

But she persisted with one more question. "Separated for a long time?"

"Five years."

"Mmm. A long time."

He finished the last of the cider in his glass and sighed. "Yeah."

Margie wished she could interpret the sigh, the sudden loss of luster to his eyes, beyond her realizing it was a sigh of finality, a termination of the subject without the need of stark words. He was very sensitive about the subject of his marriage. It didn't take words to convey to her that he wasn't going to discuss it.

Across the room, Newton snorted softly in his sleep, an utterly pig kind of sound that broke the tension and caused Kyle to smile. Angel's ear twitched. King lifted his regal head arrogantly and gazed at Newton with skeptical curiosity. The fire burned brightly, casting quivering shadows on the wall as daylight faded.

Margie felt Kyle's eyes on her, hard and soft at the same time. Beside her on the thick rug, he reached out to touch her wrist. Slowly his fingers moved down, pausing with tranquil ease before he raised her small hand slowly in his large one and pressed his lips against the back of her hand.

Drawing a breath of surprise, Margie watched him while her heart began to flutter. The warmth of his lips against her cool skin was so unexpected. The urge to touch his thick hair was strong, but shyness held her back. He brushed her hand against his cheek where the softness of his lips gave way to the bristle of his beard. The blizzard had roused him early from bed this morning; he hadn't taken time to shave.

He closed his eyes and muttered, "You're as lovely as a spring morning."

Unable any longer to resist touching him, she reached out and stroked his hair, running her fingers luxuriously through it. "And you—you are a winter twilight."

His eyes opened, but he didn't move her hand from his cheek. "Why a winter twilight?"

"There is a splash of clear, warm color, but the sky behind it is filled with shadows of darkness. Night is so close, behind the brilliance."

Kyle's brow wrinkled while he looked at her. "You're saying I have a dark side."

"Yes...."

"I didn't realize it was so obvious."

"I doubt that it is obvious, not to everyone. Sometimes I'm sensitive to ... to certain ... people."

"Perceptive," he corrected, moving his fingers gently along her forearm. "But I'm not that dark, really. Not..."

Whatever he had intended to say was lost in a deep exhalation of his breath, as if he'd lost focus of what he was thinking and his thoughts were shuffling through a whorl of shadows to the present moment and to the nearness of the woman sitting beside him on the fire-warmed floor.

His gaze fixed on hers. He moved closer, caressing her upper arm now, over her heavy pink sweater. She felt his warm touch on her neck, then her throat. Involuntarily, Margie moved back her head in an unconscious gesture of acceptance, exposing her throat fully to him. To his touch. To his lips.

Her eyes closed as his lips came nearer, brushing gently across the whiteness of her throat, her cheek and, finally, her mouth. A thrill shivered through her, caught and held her. And rendered her helpless.

At her response, Kyle's arms encircled her and he held her, prolonging the kiss. When their lips finally moved apart, he still held her for half a minute more in a strange, restive silence. Her sigh of pleasure swelled her chest against his.

"Should I..." he whispered into her hair, "should I not have kissed you?"

"What kind of question is that?"

He smiled softly. "Not a good one. If you hadn't wanted me to, you'd have let me know."

Margie thought, *this man is married, isn't he? Or is he? Five years is a long time....* Married or not, he came alone to Rosewood; he lives alone. Married or not, his kiss had a sparkling quality like diamonds that made all other kisses she'd ever known seem only imitations by comparison. And he touched her as if he were touching a priceless, fragile piece of china, almost as if—she thought—as if she were forbidden. Was she...forbidden?

Reluctantly, confused, she rose, leaving the warmth of Kyle and the fire, to look out the window.

"The wind's beginning to die down. But the drifts are over the corral fences. I can't get my little snowplow through that stuff."

He said, "It doesn't sound like a horse could get through, either."

"It looks impossible for a horse, and it's still pretty blowy out there. Sky might sink in drifts to his shoulders in some places. Let's get some news reports on the radio."

Kyle stretched out on his stomach, his bare feet toward the fire. He scratched his head. "How am I gonna get home?"

"I don't think you can."

Through the noise of a singing radio commercial, he said, "I'm stuck here for the night?"

"It looks that way, doesn't it?"

He sat up. "And that's okay with you? Sounds like the makings of a scandal."

"Are you worried about a scandal?"

He laughed.

"Good. Neither am I." It felt so good to say it, knowing that it was true. To say the word "scandal" without shivering at her memories was a kind of freedom. Once she'd worried so much about what people thought. Since those awful days, Margie had progressed in age and understanding and tolerance for her own mistakes.

Kyle's gaze moved to the opposite side of the room, where Newton lay snoozing. "Yeah, I can see why you don't worry about such things, with your trained police pig there. You don't need him tonight, though. You trust me, don't you?"

"Of course."

One eyebrow raised. "Why? When you know what kissing you does to me?"

"I have pretty good perception." She smiled. "Actually, I don't think it will be hard making the best of this storm. The spare room is already made up, and I have some nice steaks in the freezer and some popcorn for later."

"I'd say this is the way to suffer through a blizzard!" He rose from the floor. "I'll get my boots on and plow my way to the barn to make sure the horses are warm and fed. Is there anything else that needs to be done? I noticed you have plenty of firewood."

"Everything's okay...." Margie breathed, feeling a sensation of warmth as he came near her. He lightly touched her hair, then kissed her forehead.

"Thanks, Margie."

"For what?"

"For everything. For being you."

She leaned softly into his arm. "Who else would I be?"

"Someone with...hang-ups...someone...insecure. Someone less trusting."

Margie blinked up at him, afraid that the effects on her of his nearness might be evident to him, that the little trembling inside her might somehow show outside. "I'm also glad," she said in a small, self-conscious voice, "that you're you."

That night, after an evening by her fire with him on his best behavior, Kyle lay awake in Margie's guest room, tossing, trying to get comfortable, trying to sleep. The turmoil inside him had never been stronger than now, because added to the constant encumbrance of being pursued was a powerful attraction to Margie Donovan. It had been a long time since the needs within him had surfaced as they had tonight—need for a woman's softness, need for sharing, need to quell the aches and longings inside him that he had tried to keep suppressed for too long.

His life was a mess, and he didn't want to involve Margie in that mess. Yet any association with him could involve her. Across a dimly lighted hallway Margie slept behind the closed door of her room. Kyle pictured her sleeping and at peace and envied her. He'd forgotten what it felt like to be at peace.

It had been five years since Claire had flown off into the sky never to be seen or heard from again. And after five painful, frustrating, damn years, what had become of her was still a mystery—to him, to the police and to the insurance company carrying her life insurance policy.

Tonight, tossing, wishing harder than ever that he could shed the nightmare of his past, Kyle thought back to the day his wife filed a flight plan and took off in their Cessna. He had suspected almost from the moment the plane was declared missing that Claire hadn't actually flown that route at all; she'd gone another way.

Suspicions! What the hell good were suspicions? His life since that day was a tangle of suspicions. They formed strangling chains around him and the chains kept getting tighter. There was his own suspicion about Claire and another man. And then Wayne Brockmeier's suspicion that the plane was rigged and Claire was murdered. By him. Brockmeier's alternate suspicion was that the two of them could have planned her disappearance together to wait out the statute of limitations and collect their two million dollars. That damned two-million-dollar policy Claire had insisted on was likely to get him charged with murder. Now, as the statute of limitations loomed nearer, the company was stepping up efforts to pin something on him. The harassment was getting worse.

A bare branch scraped across the window of Margie Donovan's guest room in the force of wind. It had stopped snowing, but the night was very black behind the thin curtains. Kyle ground his teeth together as he lay in the dark. Neither the weight of his burden nor his anger ever lessened. He wanted rid of Wayne Brockmeier, of his marriage, of memories, and he was chained to them. Aching to be free, Kyle grabbed onto the new, thin ray of hope that his attorney's letter had meant something, that the reports about Claire's presence in Florida were more than vaporous rumors. Desperately, he wanted her to be found alive.

If she wasn't, they might go so far as charge him with murder. Lying in bed, Kyle swore aloud. His getting too friendly with Margie would mean trouble for her. Their relationship would be under scrutiny. And worst of all, she'd learn he was suspected of murdering his wife.

Kyle thought of Margie's smiling eyes and of her laughter and of the softness of her throat and her lips. He wanted her. Wanted to be near her, to hold her, to make love to her. But he couldn't allow himself to be that selfish or to tell her the sordid truth about himself. The only choice he had was to pull away while he still could.

Come morning, he'd somehow dig his way out of here and out of a situation for which he longed in order to get himself back into a situation he hated. Because he had to. On this special snowed-in day, mesmerized by the magic of the fire and by her beauty, he had already gone too far to back away from Margie without her noticing and probably being hurt. But it was going to be nothing compared to the hurt that would befall her if he didn't stop this now. He'd do it gently.

Kyle slept very little that night. He dozed and woke tired—not a temporary tired from mere lack of sleep but a bone-deep kind of tired. He was tired of the bizarre circumstances that rendered him helpless to take control of his life.

MARGIE SENSED SOMETHING secretive about him, even before she came to suspect he might be trying to avoid her after the blizzard. It had been so good—all those soft, sharing hours by her fire. So natural and so welcome had been his touch, his kiss. Yet Kyle seemed to be making himself scarce in the days that followed the storm. Twice he had dropped by to say hello, and he was friendly and laughing the way he always was. It was just that she had expected more, after their day together, than just his friendship. But there was no more. He didn't kiss her again. Unable to understand, Margie suffered twinges of regret and hurt. She thought of him more than she wanted to. Many times a day she thought of his kiss.

The ice that had been broken between them seemed to be freezing again, slowly, and she didn't know why.

Margie had no way of knowing that it would begin to melt again on one of the most embarrassing days of her life.

It was the day of the annual fund-raising fashion show in the convention room of the hotel. A modeling ramp had been installed across the front and down the center of the large room. White-clothed tables were set up on all sides for the champagne luncheon. Each shop in town furnished designs from its latest collection to be shown at this, the town's most elegant event, rivaled only by the New Year's Eve ball. For the third year in a row, Margie had been asked to model for Kate's Boutique.

That same day, a cold Friday, Sergeant Pig Newton had a scheduled engagement, too. Newton had been invited by the principal of the grade school, John Piper, to spend the afternoon with the sixth-grade class. The children had planned experiments in testing the keen sense of smell of pigs, and Newton, who enjoyed the companionship of children, was a welcome celebrity whenever he visited a school.

When Margie pulled up in front of the school, she was met at the curb by John Piper before she could get Newton down from the back of the pickup.

"We've got a problem, Margie," he said. "The fire department has scheduled a surprise fire drill for today. It hasn't taken place yet, and I'm afraid to have the pig here for that. I remember you warned that he tends to overreact and panic if people scream. And when the children start lining up and rushing about, not knowing whether the drill is real or not, I'm afraid there could be some panic. With that pig in the middle of things, there could be real chaos in a fire drill. I'd chance it, mind you, but some very important people from the state education association will be here, and I want everything to run smoothly. Things don't always go smoothly when Newton is around, as we well know. Can you bring him next week instead?"

Margie wrinkled her nose. "I guess so. I have to be at the hotel for the fashion show in fifteen minutes, though. Newton will just have to wait in the truck."

Concern darkened John Piper's face. "I thought you couldn't leave him in the back of the truck when you're in town. People make too big a fuss."

"I know. He'll have to sit in the cab."

The man scratched his head, looking guilty.

Margie smiled. "It's not that bad. Newton loves to get into the cab. He thinks he's very important sitting there. And I won't have to be in the hotel too long, just to model three outfits. It isn't vital that I stay for the luncheon."

"I'm sorry about this."

"It's not your fault. It'll be okay. Newton can sit in the cab and watch people go by. He'll enjoy himself. And as for me, I don't enjoy the conversations at lunch anyhow. All that gossip. I'll tell them I have to take my pig home and that'll give them something else to snicker about."

John Piper stood back and watched Margie set up Pig Newton's ramp so he could get down from the bed of the pickup. When the pig realized the cab door was being opened for him, he squealed his delight, jumped clumsily into the truck and, from the floor, got himself onto the seat with another squeal and a grunt. Propping himself up, he looked out of the window with an enormously pleased expression on his face.

"All he needs is a straw hat." Piper laughed.

"Knowing Newton, he'd probably wear it. Tell the kids I'll bring him back to school on Tuesday. That's a sale day, and I can pick him up after the sale."

Margie parked on Main Street in front of the hotel, where Newton could amuse himself by watching the people going by on the busy sidewalk.

"I won't be that long," she promised, as if the pig could understand everything she said. And giving him a pat on the head between his twitching ears, she got out and hurried inside. The fashion show was just getting under way.

Because it was such a prestigious event, all of Rosewood's socialites were represented at the luncheon, dressed to impress and outdazzle one another. Arrangements of white-and-red roses bedecked each table, and pink champagne bubbled in tall, stemmed goblets. Margie hurried to the small anteroom where the models were dressing.

It all went very well, at the start. Then halfway into the show, the nightmare began.

Margie was changing clothes, standing in her slip, when screams sounded from the luncheon room. With a terrible foreboding, she followed three other models to the doorway and peered out. A dozen or more carefully coiffed women had left their seats at the table and were skittering around, shrieking, trying to avoid the source of terror.

Newton.

The enormous pig was in the center of the room, upsetting chairs to get at the glasses of champagne, which he was lapping at enthusiastically.

Margie's heart sank. She yelled at him from the doorway. At the sound of her voice, the big head raised and the beady eyes peered in her direction. A loud, lewd-sounding snort rent the air. With relief, she realized he was responding to her call. Stopping for a few more slurps of champagne, he headed straight for the back room and his mistress. Margie ducked back, wriggled out of the slip and began frantically to struggle into her jeans, tripping over her pant legs in frustration. She felt perspiration dampen her armpits.

In moments, Newton was at her side, greeting her pleasantly as if to say, "Oh, here you are!" Fighting back tears, she tried reasoning with him in the midst of the shrieks of mixed laughter and horror surrounding her in the anteroom and outside, echoing from the banquet hall.

Newton hated the screams. Confused, he backed away and into a rack of hanging clothes. The wheeled rack slammed the wall, and Newton slid under it, for a moment entirely hidden by the veils of floor-length gowns. The rack tilted and rocked wildly, but miraculously it didn't fall. The pig tried desperately to free himself and turn around, but he was hampered by the fabric of a full-skirted pink chiffon gown. Showing signs of panic under the flow of pink gauze, Newton lunged away from the clothes rack, pulling the gown off its hanger as it wrapped around his wriggling snout and fell back over his head and his stiff-haired pale pink shoulders.

With his vision partially impaired by the skirt, he jogged in small, fast steps toward the door, flanks bouncing, tail twitching, emitting pig snorts with every step—snorts that Margie was mentally translating as, "Get me out of this madhouse!"

The frustrated animal trotted through the door and back into the luncheon hall. He was met by shrieks of laughter that he had no way of knowing were at his expense. The model's ramp stretched before him, the only clear passage he could see. Margie was behind him, barefoot, buttoning her shirt, but she was not in time to catch him.

The shrieks and howls had gone beyond the hall into the hotel lobby and consequently out to the sidewalk, as word spread like a windswept brushfire that disaster had struck the fashion show. A small crowd began to gather around the hotel and in the lobby.

Kyle was in the drugstore at the cashier's counter, buying aspirin and toothpaste, when he heard sounds of commotion from the sidewalk and the hotel next door. When he stepped outside, he saw Margie's pickup parked along the curb in front of the hotel with the cab door standing open. Involuntarily, he gritted his teeth. Something told him that Margie Donovan was in need of help.

He wove his way through the thickening crowd at the hotel door and into the lobby. Following the sounds of chaos from inside and ignoring the protests of the hotel manager, he pushed at the big double doors that led into the conference room.

The sight before his eyes froze him to the floor. Strutting back and forth on the model's ramp, draped in a flowing pink gown, was Pig Newton.

5

AMID THE WAILS of perfumed, matronly ladies, Kyle was gripped by a seizure of helplessness. Tears of laughter formed in his eyes. His chest contracted as laughter rose choking from his throat.

He sobered slightly when he glimpsed Margie's face at the edge of the ramp. Trying desperately to grab hold of Newton's gown as he trotted by, she was not laughing. Her face was as white as the tablecloth on which she was kneeling. A glass of champagne had spilled on her jeans and a centerpiece of roses had been knocked over, water from the vase spilling out and dripping in a steady stream onto the floor. Voices were shouting at her from all directions.

The sight of her agony dampened his enjoyment of the hilarity of the scene. Kyle rushed forward, threw his package down on the ramp and moved one of the long, heavy tables aside as easily as if it were made of cardboard, so he could get close to the ramp. As Newton sailed by, Kyle made a lunge for him, but he couldn't hold on. The pig's hind foot came down hard on Kyle's arm.

Kyle cursed in pain. More laughter rose behind him.

"Margie!" he said. "I thought this pig was trained to listen to commands!"

Her voice came shaky and weak across the ramp. "He's afraid of the...of the dress! And of all the screaming and laughing...."

"We've got to get the dress off him, then!"

"Yes," she wailed. "I've been trying! It's wrapped around his snout!"

There seemed to be a dozen layers of chiffon, flowing in all directions. Kyle positioned himself on the ramp ahead of the pig, waiting for the chance to grab him again.

From the loudspeaker, a voice boomed out. It was not the voice of the official mistress of ceremonies, who had run for cover, but a male voice that didn't belong behind the microphone at all. "And now, ladies, in a pink evening gown is a pig wearing the sensational new fashion look of the season. . . ."

"I want to die," Margie muttered as she came around the ramp toward Kyle. Her bare feet slid in spilled champagne, nearly causing her to lose her balance. "But not before I kill Newton!"

"How'd he get in here?"

"I don't know. Someone must have opened the truck door and let him out. Some kid, probably. A lot of kids know him."

Newton did an unexpected pirouette at the ramp's center and started back down. His efforts to keep from tripping on the fabric gave the appearance of strutting, if indeed it was possible for an overweight pig to walk with a strut. This time they were ready for him, Kyle on one side, Margie on the other.

The squeals were deafening. Kyle held him back as best he could while Margie untangled the filmy material from his snout and back and spoke to Newton in fierce, threatening whispers. The anger in her voice seemed to subdue him.

There was a crushing of paper and a popping, squishing sound as Newton's hoof came down on the paper sack Kyle had carried in from the drugstore. Toothpaste oozed out. The pig slid sideways in the toothpaste with a terrible squeal, stopping only after one hind foot had gone off the edge of the stage ramp.

Yanking at his ear, Margie led Newton across and through the narrow door at the back. A trail of toothpaste followed them. So did the laughter. So did a trail of curses.

The door shut behind her. She turned around. Kyle, with his arms full of pink chiffon, stood with the door secured shut at his back, simply staring at her and her pig. Newton snorted softly, his long eyelashes blinking innocently. Margie was visibly shaking.

"Lord..." was all he said.

"Oh, Kyle, I'll never live this down. People will be talking about this for the next fifty years.... Thank... thank you for helping me. No one else would because they're scared of Newton."

"*That* scared of him? Why?"

"He killed someone once."

"He what?"

"In the line of duty. He saved a sheriff's life. It's hardly fair, but now everyone calls him a killer pig and no one wants to risk getting him mad." Margie sat down to pull on her socks and boots while she looked at him helplessly. "Oh, that beautiful dress!"

He held it up. "It doesn't seem to be torn. There's a little toothpaste on it...."

Margie hid her face in her hands as if she couldn't stand any more.

He said, looking over the strapless gown, "I like this. Would it fit you? Sure it would. I can tell. I'll buy it."

"Kyle, it is—it was—a very expensive dress. I can't let you do that, just to protect me."

"I want to see you in it. You'll look a hell of a lot better than Newton. That I know for sure."

"Oh, Kyle . . ."

His eyes scanned the small room. "Isn't there any way out of here without having to go back through the ballroom and the lobby?"

"No, damn it all, there isn't. I don't think I can face walking through there . . . with Newton."

"I'll help. We can't stay in here the rest of the day."

Most of the comments were good-natured as the noisy crowd parted to let them pass. Margie was leading Newton by the ear. "Kyle," she whispered, "must you carry that dress?"

From behind the mound of chiffon, he answered, "Yep. You'll have to let me know who to write the check to."

Her voice cracked. "It looks bad enough having to escort this pig out, but with you carrying the dress Newton . . . wore . . . it's even more embarrassing."

"Hell, I don't care how it looks. It's too late to care about that, isn't it?"

With a loud, nasal oink, Newton stepped sideways to check out a bottle of spilled champagne.

"Don't you dare!" Margie growled, jerking at his ear as if the strength of her hand had any effect at all on restraining him. But the tone of her voice did, and Kyle's fast action did. He picked up the bottle, set it aside and flanked Newton on the left to discourage any further distractions. The three of them paraded through the room like dignitaries at a VIP reception, looking straight ahead and ignoring the guffaws.

Outside, at the curb, people stood around and watched, some with friendly smiles and comments, while Margie and Kyle unloaded the ramp and shooed the pig up into the bed of the pickup.

Kyle jumped into the cab beside her.

"Are you all right, Margie?"

"No. I'm shaking like a leaf. Oh, the luncheon—that beautiful luncheon—completely spoiled! And the fashion show, as well. Please tell me this is just a bad dream."

There was only silence from the passenger seat. Margie looked over at the man who sat with the enormous mound of pink fluff on his lap, leaning back in the seat, desperately trying to restrain his chuckles.

"Kyle, are you laughing?"

He sputtered and couldn't answer.

"You *are* laughing! You're *laughing!*"

He broke into raucous laughter and couldn't stop.

Margie stared at him. Gradually the anxiety on her face began to change, the tenseness in her body relaxed. A smile forced its way out. She grinned and shrugged helplessly.

"And for that special occasion, ladies," Kyle mimicked, "may we present this elegant gown of pale pink..."

"Accented with a scattering of rhinestones," Margie finished. "And falling in delicate folds over the...the snout..." She broke into nervous giggles.

Aware of people gathered around the pickup, looking at Newton, Margie said, "I can't believe you just made me laugh."

"Why not laugh, honey? What the hell else can you do?"

"Nothing, I guess. Except take this insufferable monster home and arrange to pay for damages and hope Charlotte Willis and the luncheon committee will reschedule without too grand a fuss." She grimaced. "I think my modeling days are over."

Margie turned. "Oh, just what I need. Reporters from the local paper for the story of the year."

"I'll call you later tonight," Kyle said. "If you need me just let me know."

Apologizing for the hasty exit, Kyle slid from the truck and backed away, avoiding the reporters and photographers, who were snapping pictures of the posing pig in the back of Margie's truck.

SHE SAW HIM the following day in the drugstore. He was standing before the home-remedy shelf choosing aspirin and didn't see her approach. Margie moved up behind him. "I always buy the generic brand."

His smile was spontaneous. "Hi, Margie. I'm glad to see you're not in hiding."

"There's a sale today. I have to work."

"Yeah. Me, too. I hate working Saturdays." He looked back at the pain-remedy display and picked up a box. "If you recommend the generic, it's good enough for me."

She shrugged self-consciously. "I'll bet you're buying toothpaste, too."

"How'd you guess?"

She reached behind her on the shelf and handed him a box of toothpaste.

"Hmm...this is my brand! How could you know I use this brand?"

"The little green specks in it. I use it, too."

He grinned. "Oh, the dress. Did it wash out?"

"Beautifully. It's really quite a lovely dress, Kyle."

"Wear it for me sometime."

"All right." She paused. His suggestion—just short of an invitation—was friendly but so vague. "I haven't seen you much, Kyle. I suppose you've been awfully busy."

"Yeah. Doing some work on the interior of the house— you know, painting, knocking a couple walls down, sanding floors."

When he smiled down at her, she saw something in his eyes that puzzled her—a kind of sadness that lingered for a moment, then seemed to disappear and then appear again. Margie remembered his chivalry yesterday—helping her subdue a show-off pig when no one else would help. And she remembered his kiss the day of the blizzard. A small shiver moved through her.

"Got time to have a cup of coffee with me?" Kyle asked.

"Sure."

"If you want to grab a place at the counter, I'll pay for this stuff and be right over there."

"I'll order for you. Coffee?"

"With sugar."

"Oh, yes. With sugar."

A minute or two later, when he sat down on the stool beside her at the counter, Margie felt the brush of his thigh against her thigh and it was like being hit by a soft, warm surge of electricity. Perhaps Kyle felt it, too, for he looked at her strangely, almost dreamily, the way he had looked at her just before he kissed her by the fire. He couldn't hide what was in his eyes—his attraction to her. Maybe he wasn't even trying to hide it.

He set his small package on the counter. Margie sipped a cherry cola, holding onto the straw with slightly trembling fingers. She was remembering his warmth.

"Is Newton suffering any pangs of guilt?"

"Not a one. He acts like he can't see any reason why I should be upset with him. He has crashed parties before, but taking over yesterday's society fashion-show luncheon was a star act, even for Newton. Did you see his picture on the front page of the paper?"

"Yep."

"People think it's funny, Kyle. Not the ladies' circle that sponsors this show. But other people think it's funny."

"Hell, it is funny."

She slurped her drink through the straw. "I dunno. I sure didn't sleep much, thinking about it." *I thought maybe you'd come by last night,* she thought. *But you didn't.*

As if he were reading her thoughts, he abruptly changed the subject. "I ran into Dick Campbell at the hardware store the other day. Evidently he's having a hard time living as a runner-up. He wanted to challenge me to another skating race at the first hard freeze next winter."

She raised her brows in surprise. "And did you take him up on it?"

"Hell, no. I told him I had better things to concern myself with."

"It was a big thing for Dick to be ice-skating champion of the valley. You're champion now. That may call for defending your title from time to time."

"I didn't ask for the title."

"But would you defend it?"

Kyle stirred his coffee absently. "Oh, sure, I guess so. But not with Campbell. After what he pulled, there's too much pleasure in watching him squirm."

"You could beat him again."

"Yeah," he agreed with an amused nod of his head. "I could."

Margie turned toward him in time to notice Kyle's eyes shifting from her to the window of the store. A frown formed on his forehead, so slight it was almost imperceptible. He shifted as if he were conscious of someone watching them.

Puzzled, Margie turned around. Old Mrs. Turnover was talking to the pharmacist at the counter. Two young women she didn't recognize were browsing through a display of cosmetics. A rancher in bib overalls was waiting at the cashier's counter. It was a quiet, wintry afternoon. Yet Kyle seemed restless all of a sudden.

She asked, "Is something wrong?"

"No. Why?"

"You seem distracted, as if something is bothering you."

"No. Nothing."

But something was, she could tell. Something, all of a sudden. Just as the appearance of the two reporters had bothered him yesterday.

Kyle threw a bill onto the counter and rose. "Gotta get back to work. Nice seeing you, Margie."

He exited suddenly, as he'd done yesterday, pausing in the doorway to zip up his parka before he went out into the cold, but he didn't look back. Confused, Margie watched him through the front window of the store as he crossed the street, heading toward his office in the upper floor of the bank building. He had seemed restlessly distracted when there was nothing anywhere around—that she could see—to distract him.

Several discrepancies about this man's behavior didn't make sense. She liked him more than she wanted to. He was the most fascinating man she'd ever met. Driving to the auction barn that morning, Margie Donovan reflected back on her life. Was she lonely and didn't know it—wouldn't admit it? Did Kyle stimulate emotions she had tried too hard to forget? Probably, damn it!

Was her peaceful life in Rosewood really a kind of escape from reality? It had been a long time since she had been affected like this by a man. The last time was Troi, in France. At the memory, her heart constricted. Not for Troi, anymore, but for their child who never had a chance to live. Her secret. Her scandal, so carefully guarded. Why was it, Margie asked herself, that the older she got the less it mattered what people said about her? Her pal Newton was teaching her some things about that. Another time in her life she'd have been devastated by yesterday's disaster at the fashion show. But twice since then, with Kyle, she'd actually been able to smile about it.

Maybe she wasn't hiding anymore; Rosewood was home. Maybe she was where she was supposed to be, because she was happy, genuinely happy. There were just those moments, with Kyle and thinking about Kyle, when Margie felt an unfamiliar kind of emptiness. A need to love. And to be loved.

Maybe it had been long enough. Maybe it had been too long.

SEVERAL DAYS LATER, when she was working the regular Tuesday Rosewood auction, Margie noticed Kyle in the audience. He was sitting in the top row, looking over the sales barn, the one his design would replace by the end of next summer, and when she caught his eye, he greeted her with a friendly little smile that she had to recognize as a hello and not as a bid. For a second, she lost her concentration and missed a signal. The tipping of the rim of a bidder's Stetson hat had to be pointed out to her by an assistant in the ring who was managing the livestock.

There were only horses being sold that day and it was not a long sale. Margie wondered if Kyle had come to look over the horses. If he was in the market for another horse, he didn't bid on any of these, and there were some fine animals in the ring. Or had he come to see her? If he had, he didn't wait around for her. Before the sale had ended, she looked up to discover he wasn't sitting there anymore; he had left. Margie didn't try to deny her disappointment.

She wanted to talk to him about business, if nothing else. He had promised the auction-barn committee that she, as auctioneer, would have the opportunity to look over the plans he drew. Those plans ought to be finished by now, even though Kyle hadn't said so, and she wanted to see them. She also wanted to see Kyle, under whatever excuse she could conjure up to do so. These past weeks he had been a little like a shadow—there and not there. He was so natural and friendly whenever he saw her, as though they were fast friends. He just didn't go out of his way to see her, the way she'd hoped he would.

Chancing that he'd be in his office, Margie stopped there after the sale was over. The gray sky seemed to hover just over the tops of the buildings in the small town this late afternoon. Twilight brought a chill. When she parked in front of the bank building, a glance upward confirmed that Kyle must be in his office; a light was on in the second-story window.

Dust from the sale barn clung to her jeans. She brushed herself off hurriedly when she got out of her pickup truck and was relieved to find that the entrance to the stairway leading to the upstairs offices wasn't locked.

There were half a dozen offices on the second floor, all with windows facing the street. The hallway was dimly lit with antique wall lights. The familiar stale, smoky smell of the old bank building permeated the air and stimulated memories from Margie's earliest childhood. She remembered hanging on to her father's hand while he did his banking downstairs, with conversations she never could understand, under soft clouds of cigar smoke.

Kyle's name was on the second door to the left. The door was closed but not locked. Margie let herself in.

There was no reception area, only a large desk with several stacks of papers on it, and through an alcove, by the window, stood an architect's drawing table and bench. Sketches of barn-type buildings were tacked on the walls, but generally the office had a stark, just-moved-into appearance.

From the alcove came the sound of male voices, one of which belonged to Kyle. Interrupting a business transaction wouldn't impress him favorably, she thought. Perhaps it was better to come another time.

But he had heard the door open. He appeared from around the corner. A look of surprise, bordering on shock, came over his face when he saw her.

"Kyle," Margie said. "I didn't mean to interrupt you. But I was in town—after the auction, you know—and I thought I'd drop by to—"

Two unusual things happened simultaneously. Kyle stiffened and seemed to draw back from her, giving Margie the distinct feeling she was not welcome. As he did so, another man, a stranger, emerged from the alcove sitting area, smiling a greeting at her, a much warmer greeting than Kyle's.

She looked from one man to the other—Kyle in jeans and a light blue sweater, the stranger in an olive-colored business suit and striped tie. Whoever the man was, he wasn't from anywhere around Rosewood.

"You came to look over the plans of the auction barn," Kyle said, a businesslike statement, not a question, and obviously a statement for the benefit of his client.

"Well, yes...I...but it can wait, Kyle, if you're busy."

The stranger thrust forth his right hand. "My name is Wayne Brockmeier, Miss . . ."

"Donovan," she said, wondering why Kyle was making no attempt to introduce them. His behavior wasn't far from rudeness.

"Miss Donovan. It is Miss, isn't it?"

Kyle answered before she had the chance. "Miss Donovan is my neighbor. And she's the local auctioneer, with interest in the new sales barn."

Wondering why Kyle sounded so defensive, Margie pulled back. It couldn't have been plainer that he didn't like this man, and the stranger, too, was aggressive, more subtly so, under the guise of jovial cordiality. It didn't seem likely that he was a client of Kyle's; there was too much tension in the room for any workable architect-client contract to be going on.

"How long have you known Kyle?" the man asked, pulling a cigarette from the pack in his shirt pocket and reaching for a chrome-and-bronze lighter on a side table.

Margie looked at Kyle uncertainly, noting that the stranger was scrutinizing her glance as well as everything else about her.

"Cool it, Brockmeier," Kyle warned in a voice like ice. "I won't stand for you harassing my business associates."

Margie's mind whirled. *Business associate?*

"I'd hardly call a friendly question harassment. Would you, Miss Donovan? And you did say you're neighbors."

In the presence of this man, Kyle's personality was drastically changed; he was someone she didn't know. Margie frowned. "I don't know what's going on here."

"It has nothing to do with you, Margie," Kyle said. "Just an old problem Brockmeier and I have."

"I'd appreciate an answer to my question, if you don't mind," Brockmeier said pleasantly.

"I warned you already," Kyle snarled. "Knock it off!"

"Overreaction noted," Brockmeier said, taking a heavy drag on the cigarette and backing up a step, blowing a circle of smoke into the room.

Kyle glared at him. "What the hell is that supposed to mean?"

"Just what it says. You're awful sensitive about my asking your, uh, neighbor a simple friendly question. Why so sensitive, Kyle?"

"I think I interrupted something here," Margie said in a small voice. "I'd better go. I didn't mean to—"

"I apologize for this," Kyle said.

Brockmeier thrust his hand toward her once again, this time to present her with his business card. "I'd like to question you sometime, Miss Donovan—"

"*Question* me?" she interrupted, deeply repelled by the man—by his manner and his voice.

Kyle rose over him like an angry grizzly bear. A sound like a low growl rumbled from his throat. Margie remembered his anger at Dick Campbell the night of the race. Kyle frightened her when he became this angry. He took a threatening step nearer Brockmeier; his blue eyes blazed.

Margie's heartbeat quickened. There was going to be a fight, and a bad one; she knew it. What she couldn't fathom was why.

"Kyle!" she gasped in a half breath. "What on earth is the matter with you? What's going on here?"

6

IN PANIC, MARGIE TUGGED on Kyle's arm. She might have been trying to distract a wounded bear for all the good it did her. Kyle's attention was riveted on the well-dressed stranger who had provoked his anger for a reason only the two men understood. Still her presence, her protest, might prevent a fight; she gripped his arm tightly. Awareness of her dismay began to seep into his consciousness. The tight cords in his neck began to relax slightly.

Her voice came weak and shaky through a tense silence. "Kyle..."

He blinked, swallowed and circled his shoulders as if he were winding down a spring. A glance at her frightened eyes had subdued him. For a second or two he stared at her. Then he turned. "I've lost patience with you, Brockmeier," he muttered in a low, threatening voice. "Your interfering has gone too damned far!"

The stranger's eyes narrowed, but he didn't back away. "Don't get so riled, Sanders. Hell, you're used to it. We're used to each other by now."

"This is Rosewood, not Omaha! I barely know the people in this town, and they don't know me."

Brockmeier's dark eyes were fixed on Margie while he spoke to Kyle. "You grew up not far from here, Sanders. This is home territory for you whether or not you want to admit it. My guess is you have some old friends in

Rosewood Valley. Why else would you come back here? A pretty lady maybe?"

The reference to Margie fanned the pulsing coals of Kyle's anger. He took a step nearer the other man. Margie's heart began pounding once again. *He's going to hit him!* she thought.

"You're asking for it!" Kyle muttered.

"If you hit me, I'll bring charges against you. We've been through this before."

"I don't give a damn what charges you bring. It's gonna be worth it!"

Wayne Brockmeier seemed to know Kyle well and to know when he had been pushed too far. He began to back up toward the door. "You're just making it harder on yourself," he said to Kyle while glancing sideways at Margie.

"Leave before I shove you out!"

Brockmeier looked past his would-be assailant's broad shoulders to the woman who stood behind him. "I'll be talking to you again, Miss Donovan."

It was one more goad than Kyle was willing to tolerate. He grabbed the man by the lapel of his jacket. "Get out of my office, Brockmeier!"

Fear entered the man's eyes but dissolved as soon as Kyle had let go of him. "I'll eventually get what I want," he promised as he backed out into the hallway. His voice echoed through the empty, wood-floored corridor.

Kyle's face was pale with anger as he closed the door. Margie, still trembling, waited for him to say something, but he was sullenly silent until finally he rested his hand on her shoulder and said, "I'm sorry."

"For what?"

He looked at her, then away. "For my bad manners. I have . . . I seem to have a problem with my temper."

"Yes," she said, "I know."

A silence fell.

She said, "You have more problems than just your temper, Kyle. Who is he?"

"A cross I have to bear. Just a pain, Margie. Forget him."

"Forget a man who says he wants to question me? What the devil did he mean?"

An expression of pain entered his eyes. "He's with an insurance company. If he tries to talk to you, just . . . ignore him. You don't have to talk to him."

She looked at Kyle incredulously. "He sells insurance?"

"He sells . . . trouble," Kyle mumbled almost inaudibly. He propped himself on the edge of the table. Light from the slatted window shades reflected on his face in streaks of light and shadow, gray and white. "He's an insurance investigator, Margie. He follows me like a hungry buzzard, trying to prove a case of . . . of fraud against me on an insurance claim. He can't, but he doesn't give up trying. I apologize for him."

"It sounds very serious. Why would he want to talk to me, though?"

"He's looking for an accomplice."

"What? Accomplice? That's why he said those things about you being from this area originally?"

"Yeah." Kyle sighed heavily. "He's crazy. You can easily see that. Look, let's not talk about Brockmeier. He's as paranoid as he acts. Everybody I come in contact with he harasses, trying to find this phantom accomplice, who doesn't exist. If he ever does approach you, tell him to get lost, and then please let me know about it. I'll get him off your back."

Her voice came high and weak. "How?"

"However I have to."

"Kyle. Please tell me . . ."

He wasn't willing to allow her to ask the question, because he didn't dare answer it honestly. "It's nothing I want to talk about or involve you in. I just . . . I'm sorry. Did you say you came to see the plans of the auction barn?"

She hesitated, staring at him. It was obvious from the hard line of his mouth that urging more information from him right now would do no good. He was still angry and upset and more than a little embarrassed. "Yes, I came to see the plans," she answered finally, trying to keep her voice casual. But her discomfort was acute. Kyle's behavior wasn't making sense. Neither was Wayne Brockmeier's.

He took a rolled paper from several on top of his desk and spread it out for her, holding the corners down with his palms.

"I saw you at the sale today," she said casually, her eyes on the paper.

"I was looking over the facility." Kyle cocked his head sideways. "I was also curious about the auctioneer. You're good, Margie. One of the best auctioneers I've heard, and I've heard quite a few."

She gazed at him, her eyes slightly squinting. The tightness had not entirely left his jaw, but his voice was calm now; perhaps he was forcing it to be calm. Just like that, he expected her to ignore what had just happened by pretending to ignore it himself. There seemed no choice but to try to pretend herself that something very serious had not transpired here during the past few minutes.

"Thanks . . . for the compliment," she said as her attention became absorbed by the architect's drawing spread out before her. The auction barn had similar features to the one she'd seen in Buffalo County, but there were significant differences. Several of the offices opened from the top of the arena rather than from the bottom. Below was a restaurant and space for a saddle shop, which the Rosewood committee had requested.

Kyle's finger circled over the drawing. "I'm going to expand these two offices," he said. "After looking over the barn yesterday, I decided to make these two larger and this one smaller. I'll have everything ready for final approval by noon tomorrow. Any suggestions or comments at this point are welcome. I was going to run these by your house to show them to you tonight."

"Were you?"

"Yeah." He met her eyes. "Yeah, I was."

"Well, now you won't have to." She studied the drawings. "We can use the livestock scales we already have, right?"

"Sure. The scales you have are good." Kyle couldn't blame Margie if she resented the way he had made himself scarce in the past few weeks. He had stopped by her house a time or two to say hello, but he hadn't stayed long, and he'd looked forward to seeing her tonight, with the plans. The hint of sarcasm in her voice when she'd said "Now you won't have to" stung, even though he knew why she had said it. And she was right. Why did he need an excuse to go over there?

Wayne Brockmeier was why, and Brockmeier would be looking for any hint that there was something between the two of them, any hint that Margie was part of or privy to his private life. Brockmeier never left a stone unturned, however far off the path he found it. Kyle owed it to Margie to shield her from involvement any way he possibly could. Unfortunately, the only way he knew to do that was to prevent any involvement with her himself, as far as Brockmeier could know. Today had been proof of how difficult that was going to be.

And the day wasn't yet over. As they leaned over the table looking at the plans, Kyle could smell the slightly perfumed fragrance of her hair, and he could feel the nearness of her as if warm sunshine were touching him. He remembered the warmth of her lips, remembered how her lips accepted his, how alive her heart felt, beating next to his. He wanted to be near her, near and nearer still. Being this close and trying to stay distant was going to kill him, he thought. How much was it possible for a man to put his life on hold? Everything, every emotion, every need? With a shudder, he felt the need stir in him, not a distant rumble but a pulsing, rising heat. He couldn't help himself; he wanted to be near her, to touch her . . . to make love to her.

Kyle swallowed and closed his eyes, bracing himself with both palms on the table. Even as quickly as the moment passed, Margie didn't miss it. She felt an almost imperceptible tremor sweep his body, felt his eyes move over her breasts and linger on her hair. She was aware of the strands of her blond hair that hung loose as she leaned over the table. For a moment she had the strange sensation that he was going to reach across and brush back her hair.

But he didn't touch her. Instead he straightened and waited for her to say something.

"It . . . looks superb, Kyle. I don't know how this design could possibly be improved."

"You're sure? Can you see yourself in this building, working here? Walk through a day?"

"Yes." The plans were excellent. She had looked at enough sales barns to know when one was well designed and workable. But aside from the impression of his skilled work, Margie wasn't sure of much else, because she couldn't think. Kyle was too close, and she was aware that it was their closeness that caused his body to tense, then to tremble. How the devil could she think with him so near?

Something just below the surface nagged at her. Something was very wrong.

She sighed deeply. "I'd better go."

"Why?"

"Well, because I . . . should . . ."

"Margie . . ." he cleared his throat self-consciously. "Do you think I've been . . . well, I mean . . ."

"You mean scarce? Do I think you've been scarce? Yes, a little. I'd be lying if I said I haven't wondered why. Surely it hasn't had to do with this . . . man."

Her directness took him off guard, but it also pleased him that Margie was so completely honest, even though he himself was not. "I haven't meant to be scarce."

"Haven't you?"

"Not the way you think."

"How many ways are there to be scarce?" Margie asked. "You didn't answer my question, Kyle. Does it have to do with this man who is investigating you for insurance fraud?"

"Yeah. He's a parasite that seems to need my blood to feed on. I didn't want him to connect me with you, Margie, I wanted to save you from his . . ." His voice trailed away. Then he finished, "Hell, that's only half of it. I didn't want you to know the mess I'm in."

"I *don't* know the mess you're in. Only some vague thing about suspected fraud. But you don't want to tell me, do you?"

"Not . . . right now. Sometime later I'll tell you about it."

Noting his discomfort and realizing that the fraud investigation must be very serious to be so diligently pursued, she said gently, "You're not obligated to talk about it, Kyle."

"I know. But I don't want you to get the wrong idea about me. I'm not a criminal."

She tried to make her smile look reassuring, as if she knew, of course, he wasn't. She did believe him, because she wanted to. But obviously there were people who didn't.

Kyle was watching her eyes. He rationalized: his was not the only case Brockmeier was working on; the detective couldn't stay too long in little Rosewood; and Brockmeier was only human, after all. He could be outsmarted.

"Are you sure it isn't necessary to bring the plans by your house tonight?" Kyle asked. "I'm going to make these last changes now on the office dimensions. And you might want to give some thought to them before your final approval."

She met his eyes and saw there they were smiling for the first time since she walked in the office door. "If you think I should . . ."

"I wouldn't want you to be . . . to come to any hasty conclusions about approving my plans. Is seven o'clock okay?"

"All right. I'll think about them between now and seven o'clock."

Margie turned toward the doorway through which Kyle had literally shoved a detective only a few minutes earlier. The fear-edged emotions she'd felt when she was anticipating a fistfight whirled back over her. Something more serious than Kyle let on was going on between these two men.

AT SEVEN THAT EVENING, shortly before Kyle was set to leave for Margie's, car lights shone in his driveway and he heard the crunch of tires on gravel. Brockmeier? Pulling back the kitchen shade, he saw that his first hunch was right; Wayne Brockmeier was getting out of a car and heading for the front porch.

Kyle swore under his breath and took a long time opening the door. When he finally did, Brockmeier scowled a greeting.

"It's cold out here! Were you hoping I'd freeze to death?"

"Don't give me ideas."

"You're not very careful what you say, for a man suspected of—" He paused carefully.

"Of what?" Kyle glared so threateningly that Brockmeier pulled back into a pause of silence.

It was Kyle who broke the silence. "Murder? Hell, I don't know if I'm capable of murder or not. You make me wonder sometimes. Wipe the mud off your feet, damn it. I've got clean floors."

Brockmeier looked around the rustic old kitchen. "You gave up your house in Omaha for *this*? This house is older than my grandmother and in worse shape."

"It suits me fine. It sits on good land." Kyle watched the other man unbutton his topcoat. He didn't like Brockmeier's face, never had. The eyes were a little too small and close together, the mouth a little too big. His hairline was receding enough to give him a balding look. "I don't remember asking you in."

"Look, Kyle, I'm just doing my job. You know that. I know you're sick of it, sick of me. Hell, I'm sick of you, too, but until I get some answers, you're stuck with me. I came out to see where you live. You bought this place in a blazing hurry, didn't you? Were you familiar with this ranch before you bought it?"

"Not before I found it on the market."

"That's a little hard to believe, considering how fast the deal went through."

"It was for sale. I bought it. That's not too complicated for you, is it?"

"You bought it from Marjorie Donovan."

"No kidding. Your detective skills are getting sharper every day."

Brockmeier continued to scrutinize the house. Looking at the ceiling, he said, "It'd take a lot of money to get this place modernized."

Kyle scowled at him. "It sure as hell wouldn't take two million dollars."

"Maybe you've got some cows to buy."

"I'm not a rancher. I'm an architect, and anyway, I can't see that it's any of your business."

"Everything you do is my business, Sanders. I heard a rumor this afternoon after I left your office. Heard your wife was seen in Florida. Do you know anything about that?"

"No. But if Claire is in Florida, why aren't you down there looking for her?"

"I will be when I satisfy myself that you had nothing to do with starting the rumor."

"You're nuts," Kyle muttered.

"What better way to get me off your back while you..." His voice trailed off.

"While I what?"

"This Miss Donovan. She's very attractive." Brockmeier was walking around the room, hands in his pockets.

"The rumor about Claire," Kyle said, pulling back on his trigger temper once again. "Where did it come from?"

"What I *heard* was one of her former friends, who shall for the moment remain nameless, claimed to have seen her on the street in Miami."

Kyle sighed. "That's not much."

"Reliable source, though, I think. Says she's a blonde now."

"Have you got communication with every person we ever knew?"

"To my knowledge, yes."

"How do you keep from boring yourself to death?"

"I'm determined. I think you knew about the Florida rumor."

"I didn't start it. If you're so damned smart, Brockmeier, why don't you find her? Then we could both live in peace."

"You'll stand to lose two million when I find her."

"I don't have two million now and I'm doing just fine." He took a threatening step nearer. "Look. In my opinion if you were any kind of a detective you'd have found her by now. Unless Claire is dead. I don't happen to think she's dead and I think you're stupid to be following me around instead of looking for her. Why don't you get your ass to Miami and stop wasting your time and mine worrying about my neighbors?"

Brockmeier sat down on one of the wooden straight-back chairs in the kitchen and threw his topcoat over the table. "I came to talk, Sanders. I thought maybe I'd give you one last chance to cooperate."

"*Cooperate?*"

"Yeah. Something was brought to my attention yesterday. I heard your attorney hired a private detective to look for your wife."

Kyle's laughter was less amused than bitter. "I hired a private detective five years ago. How the devil did you miss *that*?"

"I didn't, but that was five years ago. I thought then it was just for my benefit. But you've rehired him now. Why? Still trying to make yourself look innocent? Or because you heard the rumor, too?"

"Think whatever you want. I'm tired of your suspicions. In fact I'm just *tired*, Brockmeier. Don't you ever get tired?"

"No. Time is running out on me, and I don't intend to let it run out before I find out what really happened to your wife. I'll find out. I always do."

Kyle glanced at the clock on the wall. Margie would be waiting for him, and the insurance detective was showing no signs of leaving. So the Florida rumor may be more than just a rumor, after all, he thought. There might be some basis to it if Brockmeier's people had picked it up. But in that case, why wasn't the guy heading down there tonight instead of sitting here in Kyle's kitchen wasting time? Was it to assure himself that Kyle wasn't headed out of town, to Miami?

The investigator, as he had done in Kyle's office, tried to lead Kyle into a pointless, go-nowhere conversation. Kyle knew why; the man had done it before—tried to pull some involuntary information out of him, some slip of the tongue. He had checked out his home now and was in no hurry to go back out into the night's chill.

One of his worst fears had already been realized when Brockmeier encountered Margie in his office. Just her association with him was enough to cause the insurance company to check out their relationship, since they'd always believed he had an accomplice somewhere—probably a woman, a love interest.

With Brockmeier warming himself in Kyle's kitchen, sitting at the table while Kyle opened a can of dog food and set it out for King near the back door, Kyle was grinding his teeth in frustration. It must have been the Florida rumors, he thought, that brought the detective running to Rosewood now, although he'd expected him sometime soon anyway. Brockmeier never stayed away for long at a time. Kyle didn't believe for a moment that Brockmeier had heard the Florida rumors only this afternoon. He'd known before he came to Rosewood, and he hadn't mentioned it at their first encounter because he was fishing for information.

By the time the man left, Kyle was no longer in the mood to keep his promise to Margie to bring the plans to her tonight. It was late, for one thing, and for another, he suspected Brockmeier might hang around and even follow him there. Certainly that was his style. Disappointment prickled at him. He hadn't realized until now how much he'd been looking forward to seeing her. She was in his thoughts more than he wanted to admit, even to himself in solitude.

He called to say he couldn't make it and sensed her disappointment on the phone. *Damn*, he thought. *All I can be for Margie is trouble. Trouble follows me like a shadow*. He had come here to try to escape his past, yet his past just kept following him, tearing at him bit by bit until the wounds were raw—so raw he didn't think they would ever heal.

MARGIE HUNG UP the phone with a sinking feeling of something very wrong. Kyle's voice had sounded strange, and his behavior in his office this afternoon had been even stranger. Almost bizarre. She'd thought he might explain about it, about Brockmeier, this evening when he came to bring the plans. Now he'd found still another reason to avoid her. And yet she felt certain he didn't *want* to avoid her.

Angel let out a sharp yip and ran toward the door. Newton's ears pricked up and wiggled, but he didn't rise from his comfortable place on the floor. Moments later Margie heard the sound of a car on her gravel drive.

If that was Kyle coming after all, she thought, he must have made a wild dash out the door in order to get over here this soon, and that didn't make sense, since he'd phoned to tell her he wasn't coming. No, it had to be someone else, one of her other neighbors.

Without hesitation she answered the knock, then stood back in shock to see Wayne Brockmeier standing on her front porch.

7

BROCKMEIER WAS RUBBING his chilled hands. "I'm sorry to stop in unannounced like this, Miss Donovan. But I was just next door at Kyle's, and it's such a short hop over here, and I wanted to talk to you."

Her eyes squinted with suspicion. "About what?"

"About Kyle Sanders."

"I barely know Kyle Sanders."

"Yes, so he says. Can I come in? Just for a few minutes?"

"I'm really rather busy."

Brockmeier stomped his feet and hunched inside his coat. "It won't take long, I promise. It really is freezing out here. My feet are about frozen off."

No one in Rosewood Valley let another human being stand in the cold when a warm fire burned inside. It was part of Margie's upbringing and part of her. To be rudely inhospitable, even to a man like this, was unthinkable.

She stood aside, without smiling, and Brockmeier entered the living room. Met by a pink, snorting wall, the man drew back in alarm, pushing the door shut involuntarily behind him. "What the hell is this? A *pig*?"

"My pet watch pig," Margie answered casually.

"*Watch* pig? It was your pig that everybody was talking about in town today, wasn't it? Some big pig ran out on stage at a beauty contest. I saw the picture on the front page, but it couldn't have been *this* vicious-looking animal!"

"It was this pig," Margie said stiffly. "But it was not a beauty contest. It was a fashion show."

The man remained frozen against the door. "What is it doing in . . . in . . . ?"

"In my house? I told you, he's a guard pig, but you can let your breath out, Mr. Brockmeier. He won't hurt you if you don't do anything to upset him."

Brockmeier was breathing heavily as he gazed down at the pig, his body as rigid as wood. "Like what? What upsets him?"

She shrugged. "He'll let you know."

"Look, I only—"

"There's a chair by the fire," she interrupted, motioning him on into the room. "I can't imagine what you could want to discuss with me about Kyle Sanders."

"I see you like to get right to the point." He sat on the chair and unbuttoned his coat.

She sat opposite him. "It was obvious you and Kyle don't like each other. After you left I asked him who you are and he said you're an insurance investigator."

"That's right. I gave you my card." He reached into his pocket and pulled out another, which he held in front of her. "Did he tell you what case I'm investigating?"

"No. Only that it had to do with him. He said you'd be trying to question me, though I can't fathom why, and he suggested I didn't need to answer any of your questions."

"That's right, you don't have to. Not at this point. In court, though, you wouldn't have the choice."

Margie sat back in feigned relaxation. "That sounds pretty ridiculous, considering I don't even know what . . . what sort of fraud it is you suspect him of."

Brockmeier looked around the room. The pig and the dog had settled themselves on the floor, but the eyes of both animals were riveted on him. He turned back to their mistress. "Mind if I smoke?"

"No. There's an ashtray there." She waited while he lit his cigarette. The man had just left Kyle's house; this must have something to do with Kyle's not coming. Surely, though, Kyle hadn't thought Brockmeier would call on her tonight or he'd have interceded. Surely he would have . . .

Brockmeier took a small notebook from his shirt pocket, flipped it open and studied it for a moment while smoke rose into the air over his head. "You were born here in this house, is that right?"

"Yes."

"The ranch has been Donovan property for three generations, I'm told. Until you recently broke it up into sections and sold all but this one. Why did you decide to sell?"

"I'm not a rancher, Mr. Brockmeier. I never intend to become one, so what need do I have for several thousand acres of range land?"

"Then you don't intend to stay here?"

She frowned. "Of course I intend to stay here! I live here. I've got thirty acres in the section where my house sits, which is more than enough for anybody who just enjoys country living." She paused, looked down at her hands and then up at him. "And suppose I *didn't* intend to stay here? Of what concern could that possibly be to you? Why the devil have you been investigating *me*?"

He chose to ignore the latter part of her question. "I thought maybe your breaking up the land and selling it was an indication you weren't going to remain permanently in Rosewood. It's rare for people out here to part with land their ancestors have pioneered."

"I have no heirs to leave it to."

This statement seemed to surprise him. "You're a young woman. You might end up with plenty of heirs."

She bristled. Sadness stabbed at her at being forced to remember that she *would* have no heirs, no children, ever again.... Her voice turned ice-cold. "Why should my future concern you in the least?"

"Your *plans* for the future concern me. But not unduly. It's your past I'm more interested in at the moment."

Kyle had said Brockmeier was looking for an accomplice. It was so ridiculous. No one could link her past to Kyle's when there was no link.

"You had relatives in Wheedlin, Nebraska, a great-aunt and uncle. They owned a feed store there."

"They've both been dead for several years."

"Yeah. But when you were a kid you used to visit them."

She only stared at him.

"Wheedlin is the nearest town to the ranch were Kyle Sanders grew up. Small place. You must have met there, known each other."

"Don't be silly. I was rarely in Wheedlin, only once in a while in the summer. I never met Kyle until after he had bought the grove section of my ranch."

"Never, huh? You never met at the University of Nebraska? You were both enrolled there at the same time."

Margie smiled. "It's a huge university! I couldn't have met more than a tiny fraction of the student body. It is impossible to take this seriously, Mr. Brockmeier. I realize you're trying to convince yourself I've known Kyle for several years, but—"

"I'm convinced you have," he said. "When enough small 'coincidences' accumulate, it is enough to assume they aren't coincidence. I'm thinking about a certain summer six years ago. You were in Europe. So was Kyle Sanders."

Her gaze was incredulous, her voice viciously sarcastic. "Oh, Europe is a small place, too, isn't it, Mr. Brockmeier!"

He grinned. "I could count on the fingers of one hand the number of people from this rural county who have been to Europe. As nearly as I can determine, both of you were in France at the same time. I figure you arranged to meet there."

Margie rose from her chair. "Kyle called you crazy. It must be true. I don't believe I'm hearing this!"

He was unruffled. "Sanders and his wife headquartered in Amsterdam all that summer. They took several trips around Europe together, but he also took several trips alone."

Studying architecture, Margie remembered. But there had been no mention of his wife.

"For years I've suspected that there was something more going on in Europe than I knew about because he took several trips without his wife. But I could never make any connection with anyone. Now I learn you were there."

"That is stretching coincidence so far it's laughable, and you know it."

"Sure, I know it. But I haven't finished my investigation yet."

Margie's blood ran cold through her veins. He meant an investigation of *her*, didn't he? *Didn't he?* Oh, Lord... He was scrutinizing her every glance, every tiny reaction. She fought to hide her horror and her fear.

"If you only knew how foolish you sounded, Mr. Brockmeier."

He sucked hard on the cigarette and blew out a great puff of smoke. "I know my job. When there's a murder investigation, we follow every lead no matter how unrelated it may seem at first."

Her face went pale. *"Murder?"*

He watched her. "We can't call it murder officially yet, but—"

"Whose murder?"

The man continued to smoke in silence, his eyes intense on her. "You don't expect me to believe you don't know?"

"Kyle didn't say anything about murder. He said—" her voice lowered "—fraud."

"Oh, yes, fraud. Officially, so it is."

"Whose murder?"

"Kyle's wife."

Margie turned her face from his so he couldn't see her reaction. The heat of the fire was hot on her skin but not as hot as the fire that shot up from within her. Kyle had said they were separated, not that his wife was dead. Something here was wrong, terribly wrong.... Would Kyle lie to her? Would Brockmeier? She didn't dare ask too many questions. But she heard the echo of Kyle's voice saying "I'm not a criminal." She heard the beating of her own heart, believing him when he said it, and her heart believed it still. "Kyle's wife is dead?" she asked when she could find her voice. "You surely don't suspect him of . . . killing her?"

He looked at her indulgently as if to say he was impressed with but not fooled by her acting. "You know, of course, that Kyle stands to collect two million dollars from my company unless I can prove it was murder."

Her lips drew back in a scowl. So that was it. Life insurance. Kyle's wife must have died under suspicious circumstances. Why wouldn't he have said she was dead? Brockmeier was lying! She was sure of it. Margie forced calm into her voice. "You think he's a murderer and you think I'm involved. You actually think I'm involved in murder because the man who bought a section of my land vacationed in Europe the same summer I did! I don't believe this. I'm probably dreaming it."

Brockmeier crushed out his cigarette and immediately lit another. "Why were you in Europe?"

"Why does anybody go to Europe?"

"Most people go to tour, to see as much as they can in as short a time as possible, so they can say they've been everywhere. But that doesn't seem to be the case with you. From what I've gathered, you spent most of your time in France."

How the hell do you know this? she wanted to scream. It was easy to understand Kyle's hate for this man. Margie stiffened and set her jaw tightly, not wanting to lose her temper as Kyle had done. Instinct told her losing her temper would only verify for him his suspicions. "That's not true," she said. "I toured . . . quite a lot."

"You went to France alone."

"Yes. One of my sorority sisters in college was from France. I stayed with her family."

"You speak French?"

"What little I did pick up, I've forgotten." She turned. "I hope you're finished, because I've lost all interest in this conversation. What I did on a summer vacation years ago has no connection whatever to Kyle Sanders or to anything that could possibly relate to . . . to the death of his wife. I resent the implication that it could, and I refuse to discuss it anymore or answer any more of your stupid questions." She paused, and her voice lowered. "They really are stupid questions, you know."

He rose and began buttoning his coat. "Perhaps they are, Miss Donovan. But somehow, I don't think so. I thank you for the warmth of your fire on such a cold night. One thing I've noticed about Rosewood—people are polite as hell."

"Usually we've no reason not to be."

He started for the door, aware of the eyes of the German shepherd, who rose when he did, and the pig, who stared with alert curiosity without moving his head from the pillow on the floor. "We'll talk again, Miss Donovan."

"I don't know to what purpose."

"I'm rushed these days. I have to fly down to Florida first thing in the morning. But I'll be back. How soon depends on what my investigation turns up in the next couple weeks."

Margie wanted to ask him what Florida had to do with anything, but she wouldn't. All that was important at the moment was getting this man out the door, out of her house and out of her life. She could ask Kyle about Florida; Kyle certainly would know. There were a great many things she wanted to ask Kyle. And she could now. She *had* to now. The word "murder" hung in her mind and would not let go, like a black cloud of fog blown in from some dark corner of hell.

SLEEPLESS, MARGIE LAY in the dark that night. Wayne Brockmeier had made it plain he intended to learn more about her private life, her past life . . . her months in Europe. If he did, as thorough as he seemed to be, he'd uncover the secret she had so carefully guarded all these years.

Troi. He was the part of her life she wanted to forget. For long periods now, she did forget Troi and her time in the south of France—not a summer, as Brockmeier apparently believed, but more than a year. Summer of love, autumn of fantasy, winter of disillusion, summer of pain... Scandal, regret, death. Troi had left her when their baby died, left her alone with only the pain. Yet she knew he'd have left her anyway. He never would have married her; his family, steeped in the traditions of European aristocracy, would not have stood for it.

The citizens of Rosewood, Nebraska, never changed. In that year—that one year away—Margie had changed, but no one in Rosewood ever knew. If they had, they would never have welcomed her home, never have accepted her back. She would not have been one of them any longer, if they had ever known. The town would have rocked with the scandal.

Thinking about it, about Brockmeier's damned investigation, Margie began to shiver. Time had a strange way of standing still in the valley she called home. Scandals of fifty years ago were still discussed as if they happened yesterday. If the truth about her were ever discovered here, it would never be the same. Her name would forever be associated with whispers of some mysterious Frenchman... and a baby out of wedlock....

Her mistake.

Her first and only love. It seemed so long ago now.

Brockmeier was bound to find out. And what then? Would it be all over the valley? Tossing restlessly, Margie didn't want to think about Troi, now or ever. He was gone and it was finished and it could never have been any other way. But the pain had been slow to heal.

Now there was Kyle. She thought about his warmth and his touch and imagined him beside her in the dark, talking to her, explaining that this murder investigation was a horrible mistake, a lie. Why would Kyle say he was separated from his wife if she was dead? What kind of sense did that make?

Kyle was in trouble. He'd tried to protect her from exactly what had happened tonight, and it hadn't worked. She wondered if Brockmeier had shared his suspicions about their past connection with Kyle, suspicions based on his digging into *her* past. No, he couldn't have, or Kyle would have been right on his heels tonight, following Brockmeier to her house and probably punching the man out.

The trouble he was in was responsible for his being out of reach to her because Kyle thought he shouldn't get too close. It didn't matter now. Brockmeier had already found her and acted on his runaway imagination. Only imagination.

If the case were simple, Kyle would have been charged with something. Kyle's wife must have been murdered and the insurance company suspected him. But where were the police? If Brockmeier was telling the truth, why weren't any lawmen helping him? Kyle wasn't a murderer; of this Margie was certain. *Perhaps*, she thought, *Kyle will talk to me now. Now that I'm involved up to my ears.* She had to reach out to him. The only way to learn the truth was by making the effort to drag it out of Kyle.

Tomorrow.

TOMORROW. That April morning spring came to Rosewood Valley. Winter had lingered through March and even into early April. The day before had been gray and chilly and the night cold. But when Margie woke on April 14, she woke to springtime.

It was in the air. Sunshine penetrated the stillness, thawing the last of the frosty mornings. The ache that had moved through her body in the moments of waking lingered as she stepped out of bed to pull open the curtains. Ache of remembering last night and the reverberating words that remained with her from the darkness. Murder. Scandal.

But what she saw and felt at her window served to eclipse the ache. Tulips were pushing through the newly soft earth already, impatient and anxious. Here was color again! Flowers again. Sounds of summer birds again. The feeling of newness, of being wildly alive . . . Spring. Finally, spring!

The animals sensed it, too. Newton and Angel were in her room to greet her.

"Listen to the birds!" she exclaimed, knowing that both her pets were already doing just that. Animals knew about spring, about the end of the long winter. The very earth seemed to vibrate in anticipation.

This morning was a good omen overpowering so many bad ones, she thought. The birds were singing not about despair but about love. And if they weren't, then they should be.

Now, in the bright light of morning, Margie made a desperate effort to shed her fear and confusion. Kyle, after all, didn't know about Brockmeier's visit to her and it would be far better if he didn't know about it for a little while at least. He would get upset and angry, and she was afraid of what he would do if he got too angry. What she wanted right now was information, not trouble.

Standing at her window, feeling the feather warmth of sunlight, Margie realized what she had forgotten last night in making her decision to talk to Kyle and try to draw him out. This was a working day. His office was a lousy place for private conversation; she'd discovered that fact yesterday. Her tiny office at the auction barn would be no better.

Newton and Angel led her impatiently through the house, both more eager than usual this morning to get outside to the sunshine. Margie prepared coffee and made her way to the shower while the coffee maker growled and sputtered.

Shedding her flannel pajamas was like shedding a winter coat. With a gesture of abandon, she tossed them into the laundry basket, wondering what changes might come about in her life before the chilly autumn night came when she would get them out of the drawer again. With a shudder, she fought off the thought of Brockmeier digging into her private past in order to link her with a murder. A feeling of helplessness came over her. It wasn't easy admitting it, but she was afraid of Brockmeier. Kyle may be the suspected criminal, but every instinct told her which of the two men was more dangerous. She wanted almost desperately to reach for Kyle's protection from Brockmeier.

Strange reactions, she told herself, considering Kyle had lied about his wife being dead.

She knew he was an early riser. The day of the blizzard he'd been out in the barn before six o'clock, and when he slept at her house that stormy night, he'd been up long before dawn. It would be important not to let him know too soon that anything was wrong. Forewarned, he might draw back into the caverns of secrecy and find another excuse not to talk to her.

Dressed in her jeans and a fresh white shirt, Margie poured herself coffee and went to the phone. Although it was barely past seven, he answered at once.

"Hi," she said.

"Good morning."

Margie's hand, holding the receiver, went a little weak at the sound of his voice—so deep and full and strong. She said, "Guess what day it is."

"Wednesday."

"Besides Wednesday."

He paused, then answered, "It's spring."

"You got it! Have you been outside yet?"

"Yep. I just came in."

"Kyle . . ."

"Yeah?"

"It's too nice a day to work. I don't want to go to work this morning."

There was amusement in his voice. "You called to tell me that?"

"Yes."

"Well, I couldn't agree with you more. If we lived in earlier days, there'd be spring rites today. Maypole dances and races down the hillsides . . ."

"I know. Is your work schedule such that you can't take part in the rites of spring?"

Kyle hesitated. Somehow she'd known he would.

She waited a few seconds and then asked, "Are you afraid of me?"

His answer came fast and sure. "No, pretty lady, I'm not."

"I know you're not afraid of anything else. I know you at least that well. Are you going to find an excuse not to go for a walk with me this morning in the sunshine?"

"I don't want to look for an excuse," he said honestly, and there was something else in his voice besides the honesty, something like sadness.

Something, she thought for the hundredth time, something wrong. She knew now—there was plenty wrong! "Does that mean I can expect you for coffee?"

The hesitancy was gone when he answered, "Sure."

"You could, uh, bring those plans. I'll take a couple of minutes to look at them and we'll call it a morning's work."

"I like your style."

"See you soon, then."

"As soon as I shave and shower."

Margie hung up the phone with a relieved sigh. It had worked. She had managed to break through some barrier with her insistent phone call; she could feel it. But there was a far more tangled barrier to get through. Whether Kyle liked it or not, she was involved in the tangle through the paranoid suspicions of an obnoxious detective who seemed to make a career of following Kyle around.

Today was sunshine. Promise of spring. Promise of Kyle's company. It should be a day of abandon, of finding joy just in knowing each other. It should be...if there were not dark clouds of secrets moving across the face of the sun.

On her freezer shelf were cinnamon rolls she had baked from scratch and frozen. Soon they were heating in the oven.

Kyle came to the back door, calling through the screen. "I followed my nose to the kitchen!"

"Come in!"

"What about this pig sniffing at the door wanting in?"

"Just shove him out of the way. He'll have to stay out."

Off in the distance, the two dogs were barking. Angel and King were running together this morning and had obviously found something, probably a rabbit, to chase.

Kyle smiled. "Your phone call was a surprise this morning. I thought you might be put out with me for not coming over last night like I promised."

"You had your reasons. I knew that."

When he caught her gaze, she saw the same sadness in his eyes that she had heard earlier in his voice.

"Margie, I . . ." His voice scraped with discomfort and faded. He dismissed Pig Newton with a gentle shove and a pat on the fat rear, pushed past him and paused in her doorway, taking in an enormous breath. "There's nothing better in the world than the aroma of cinnamon rolls and coffee!" He followed Margie from the back porch into the kitchen, where he set the architect's plans, rolled and held with two rubber bands, on the countertop. "Can I help with something?"

She lifted the pan from the oven. "Sure. You can eat these while they're hot."

"With pleasure!"

Plates were already set out on the small, round kitchen table. Margie poured the coffee, set out a dish of fresh butter and sat down across from him.

Sunbeams streamed in through the east window, lighting Kyle's face and dancing from his hair, piercing it with streaks of gold. His shirtsleeves were pushed up to the elbow, exposing a tan not completely faded from the hot days of last year's summer. No woman, she thought, could help but marvel at the beauty of him.

Moments later, from the depths of a silence, she remembered her manners. "I'm sorry. Was I staring?"

He picked up his coffee mug. "Was *I*?"

"What?"

"The way the sun is shining on your hair reminds me of sun shining on pale yellow flowers. Have I ever told you how beautiful you are?"

She stared at him. "I was just thinking something very much the same about you."

This brought a scoff of laughter. "Me? Beautiful?"

"Yes," she answered without smiling. Her stomach rumbled with dread of what she had to ask him.

He gazed back at her; his brow was creased at first, then gradually relaxed. His eyes closed for a second or two, and his chest heaved in a sigh. Margie would have given a lot to read his thoughts, but she said nothing. The magic of this moment should keep renewing itself the way the sun's rays kept streaming in from the window as the sun grew hotter in the sky. But instead the magic would stop all too soon when he learned why he was really here.

He remembered to eat. To be polite, she ate, too, not wanting to, not able to think much about food or anything besides the sun in his hair and the softness in his eyes when he looked at her. And his secret. Sunshine and darkness, all mixed and swirled together.

There was acceptance in his eyes now—acceptance of the moment, of their being here together, acceptance of her as his friend, at least. He wasn't fighting it anymore and his eyes said so.

I can do this, Margie told herself. *I can talk to him. But not right now, at breakfast. Later, a little later . . .*

MUD FROM THE MELTED SNOW had dried along the banks of the creek, and the ground was soft under their feet as they walked. There were signs of impatient spring everywhere, as if the earth were swelling with new life. The water was flowing with a new, free song; green sprouted from the spongy soil, and twigs of tree branches were already showing buds.

"Look," she said as they walked a hoof-pounded path under massive cottonwood trees. "I can fit my boot heel completely inside yours. . . ."

"And I," Kyle said softly, "can fit your hand completely inside mine."

She felt the warmth of his hand around hers, squeezing lightly, and he was right. Her hand fit perfectly inside his. Her hand was quickly warmed by his, and the warmth spread all through her and settled, quite comfortably, in her heart.

Kyle said, "Margie, about yesterday. I owe you an explanation for acting so...unreasonable in my office and for not coming by last night."

"Yesterday..." she repeated with a shudder.

He felt the shudder and instantly knew something was wrong. A sense of dread descended on him. Drawing a deep breath, he said, "That idiot Brockmeier drove out to my house last night, as if he hadn't already given me enough trouble for one day."

"Yes," Margie said softly. "I know."

His stomach went weak. *How could I have been so stupid!* Kyle thought. *I'll kill him!* Nervously, he brushed his hand through his hair and all he could say was, "Damn it, Margie. Damn!"

An awful silence descended over them. Silence that washed away the sounds of birds and of insects and of cattle mooing in the distance.

At length he forced himself to look at her. "I'm sorry. I didn't think he'd move that fast. I figured he'd need time to do some digging around before he confronted you."

"Digging around about me, you mean."

"Yeah. Trying to find something in our pasts to connect us."

"He had already done his digging. Obviously he's had his eye on you . . . and on me . . . for some weeks."

Kyle's eyes closed. He opened them only with reluctance. The dread was beating at his insides, barely under the surface. What the hell had Brockmeier told her? It was possible he'd told her nothing. With Brockmeier, one never knew what to expect.

He swallowed. "Well, at least there *is* no way Brockmeier could connect us. His damned probing into our acquaintance would come to nothing about as soon as it began."

Margie kicked at the dirt with her foot. She wanted to grasp his arm to give her something to hang on to because she was frightened of the future—of what Wayne Brockmeier could do to them. To her as well as to Kyle. But she didn't grasp his arm; she was afraid of the truth, too. Kyle had told her he was married. What had happened to his wife?

"You're wrong," she said.

"Wrong about what?"

"Brockmeier's probing didn't come to nothing. He did find a connection—what he is convinced is a longtime connection—between us."

Kyle stopped dead still and stared at her.

"That's impossible, Margie!"

"It's true."

Kyle paled. "I don't understand. What did he tell you?"

Margie kicked at the dirt again. "Indirectly, he accused me of conspiring with you to murder your wife."

8

KYLE'S DEATHLIKE SILENCE frightened her. Margie could hear only her own heart pounding against her chest. Through the stillness, she began to feel his seething anger. Silent, ice-cold rage. His breathing changed. She was acutely aware of his desperate struggle for self-control.

"I don't believe this!" he muttered finally, through gritted teeth.

"I couldn't believe it, either."

"I'll kill him!"

Margie drew slightly away. Her voice became pleading. "Kyle . . . ?"

"My wife isn't dead," he said abruptly.

Her beating heart slowed almost to a stop. "I don't . . . understand! I mean, I sensed Brockmeier was lying, but—"

"She's missing. There's no proof that she isn't still alive. I think she *is* alive. I know she's alive." He turned to her. "I don't know what rot Brockmeier told you, Margie, but this time he's gone too far."

"He really believes you murdered your wife, Kyle."

"I don't know what he really believes. He thinks it's a possibility because he hasn't been able to find her in five years of searching. He's convinced that either I arranged her death or that she and I together arranged her disappearance."

"To collect two million dollars' worth of life insurance."

"I see he didn't leave out anything."

"He left out everything. What happened, Kyle? Did she . . . leave you?"

"She flew off in our private plane. Filed a flight plan and never reached her destination. No search ever turned up a trace of the plane. I think she planned it, but I don't know why. I can't for the life of me fathom why, although I had suspected for some time that she was in love with another man. She's somewhere living a new life with another man; I'm sure of it."

Margie's voice was only a whisper. "How strange . . ."

"It's damned strange. And the insurance company knows it. They can't accept the fact that I'm not behind her disappearance because I'm the one who stands to collect the damned money. If no one finds Claire in the next two years, the statute of limitations runs out and she'll be officially dead. That's why Brockmeier is so determined to prove I murdered her."

"How could you have if she was lost in a plane?"

"I could have tampered with the plane. But it's a very weak theory because the plane wasn't found. In fact, it's so weak it's ridiculous. You can see it's ridiculous, honey. Brockmeier is about to find himself in a lawsuit. I've had it with him. Accusing you is the last straw!"

"He didn't actually accuse me. Not in words." Kyle was telling the truth, she knew. Brockmeier had proved last night that his reasoning was outside the perimeters of logic.

"How the devil could he even *think* you'd be involved?"

Margie smiled nervously. "It's so crazy. It seems my aunt and uncle lived in your hometown. And you and I were at the university at the same time. And we were in Europe the same summer."

He waited.

She said. "That's it."

"That's it?"

"He's sure we've known each other for years. Even secretly met in Europe when you were there with your wife."

He became silent again, overpowered by disbelief, until he muttered, "I'm sorry. What can I say, except I'm sorry?"

"You tried to prevent this, didn't you? By staying away from me."

"Obviously it didn't work. As usual, I underestimated Brockmeier."

"You won't stay away from me now, will you?"

"I don't want you hurt any more, Margie. It might be better—"

"No, it wouldn't be better! I'm already involved, and frankly, I'm a little scared of . . . of what's going to happen."

"Honey, nothing can happen. Claire isn't dead. I know it. And they can't prove any link between us when there wasn't one."

"But Brockmeier's digging. I don't like someone digging into my past."

Kyle halted, fell once again into a deep silence and rubbed his forehead as if he were in pain. This was worse than he thought, then. Much worse. It took some time before he could bring himself to look at her. When he did, he detected a subtle sheen of tears at the edges of her eyes. Tears reflected in sunshine. Tears she was probably unaware that he could see.

She, too, had secrets. And she had a right to keep them. Kyle felt guilt form into a sick feeling at the bottom of his stomach. Guilt combined with helplessness.

It was too late to stop this now. And too late for words to do any good. He reached to her and pulled her gently into his arms and held her.

At once his warmth spread through her body. There was strength in his warmth, and safety. And unspoken understanding. In his embrace, she knew that Kyle would never judge her. And she knew that he believed she would never stand in judgment of him, either. It was just that way between them. It never occurred to Kyle that she wouldn't believe him, trust him. It never occurred to her, either. Both now were victims of the same misplaced conspiracy. But somehow fate had brought them together because they were meant to be together. And this moment, in the trust of each other's arms, both felt it. Knew it.

The dozen questions about his wife's disappearance fell unasked, for the moment unremembered. Reality was the beating of his heart against hers and the hard, protective wall of his body between her and the rest of the world. He said nothing, only held her. Slowly, they began to be aware again of the soft breaths of spring around them, the chirping of birds and the singing of the little stream. And still he held her.

He whispered, "I feel as if I *have* known you for a long time. Maybe forever. It feels so natural to be close to you."

"I know. I feel the same."

"Did you know we're being followed?"

She turned swiftly. "Followed?"

"By a fat, snorting pig."

"Oh. My bodyguard."

"He's doing a lot of oinking back there. What's his problem?"

"Newton gets a bit suspicious of physical contact."

"Is that it? What would he do if I . . . kissed you?"

"I don't know."

"Let's find out."

His lips brushed hers, and the snorting bodyguard was immediately forgotten. Only the response of her heart mattered, and her heart was swelling with longing to be even nearer him. Nearer and nearer still.

Margie lost herself as part of her rose out of her body, swirled about and then came swirling back inside, settling in her stomach and her loins, though the swirling sensations wouldn't stop. The sensations left her weak, completely helpless, but she didn't care. The sensations, so new and incredibly powerful, were the manifestations of surrender. She wanted him. Needed him.

From the beating of his heart against her and the rising and falling of his chest, she knew that he, too, was surrendering to the kiss, to what they had found together, to his own needs and hers.

Unmeasured time passed in the enchantment, before the chilling squeal split the air and Kyle jerked suddenly sideways. Emitting a breathless oath, almost tripping because he wasn't well enough balanced when the assault came, he met the threat of tiny, beady eyes with a threat of his own. "Newton, you're a swine! I ought to kill you for that."

Margie had snapped abruptly to attention when Kyle was knocked off balance by the pig. Kyle's muttered threat made her laugh, for which she promptly apologized. "You wanted to know what would happen if you kissed me in front of Newton. Now you know. I think he's more jealous than protective."

"It all comes out the same. How do we get rid of him?"

Margie gazed at her pet, who was at her side now, keeping vigil on her safety. "You're a great help, Newton. See what you've done? Kyle called you a swine."

"Can't he find a mud hole to play in or something?" Kyle asked while he gazed at the twitching ears and staring little eyes of the pig.

"Mud hole? Newton hates to get dirty." She looked up at Kyle. "I'm sorry he interrupted...."

"Not as sorry as I am."

"Yes, I think I'm as sorry as you."

He took her hand gently. "Do I have to strangle a swine with my bare hands just to kiss you?"

"We might entice him into the barn and shut him in there."

"Good plan. Let's go for it."

They turned back and walked in the direction of the house and the barn.

"Not too fast," she warned. "He's already suspicious."

"How could he be?"

"Don't forget, he's a trained detective."

This comment brought a scowl. "I'm allergic to detectives."

"Yes," Margie acknowledged. "I think I am, too."

She studied him as they walked. Tree branches swayed above them, making soft shadows on his face. "I hope you don't ever get angry at me. You're frightening when you're mad."

"I'd never get angry with you."

"How do you know you wouldn't?"

"I know what makes me angry. And I know you. You're not underhanded."

"Are you sure? I had underhanded motives for keeping you away from work this morning."

"Hardly underhanded. After what Brockmeier told you, you had to talk to me. I only wish you'd called me last night after he left so you wouldn't have had a night of wondering. Or better, while he was still there. Did he actually tell you my wife was murdered—as though it were a fact?"

"Yes, he did. And accused you of the murder."

"The bastard should be off the case. This has become a personal vendetta for him. He thinks I'm outwitting him and he can't stand not being able to figure out how. It's a nightmare, Margie, the whole thing. I wanted to tell them to keep their damned money and drop the investigation, but my attorney wouldn't let me do it. He said the insurance company would try to prosecute anyhow. But do we have to talk about that now, with this fantastic spring morning all around us?"

"No. We can talk about the spring morning if you'd rather. There will soon be tadpoles in the pond and buds on all the trees and wildflowers blooming everywhere. That hill—" she pointed to the left "—will soon be full of purple and yellow flowers, and down by the house are lilac bushes. Spring is exciting. So full of miracles."

"You yourself are spring," he said. "So young and full of anticipation for new things, for good things . . . even when you're confronted with such bad things. Being with you makes me feel younger than I've felt in ages."

"You can't be very old. How old are you?"

"Thirty-four. How old are you?"

"Twenty-seven. Are you surprised? I know I look younger than I am. You look younger than you are, too."

"I don't see how I could. Sometimes I feel very old."

They had reached the barn entrance. Newton balked. Although Margie had furnished him with fine, comfortable quarters in the barn, the pig had always acted insulted by the implication that he should bunk in the barn while the canine family member, who he seemed to feel was far less clever and deserving than he, had the privilege of staying in the house.

Now Newton sensed a plot against him. The unpredictable humans had pulled this on him before—trying to get him into the barn. He stood in the doorway snorting stubbornly.

"Maybe he'll follow us inside," Margie suggested.

But he didn't. He merely watched with a superior turn of his head as the humans walked farther into the shadows of the barn's interior.

"I don't believe that pig," Kyle said. "I've always known pigs were smart, but this one is determined to prove he's smarter than we are." He turned and glared at Newton. "All right, you gargantuan bully, we'll see who gets outsmarted." Swiftly, he moved forward and slammed the door shut, leaving the surprised and grunting Newton outside.

With the closing out of the bright frame of light from the doorway, the barn was swallowed in deeper shadows. The sweet smell of fresh hay was like perfume in the air, and the silence of the big, empty building came down over them softly and thickly.

Margie looked at him. "I don't think this was quite how the plan was supposed to work."

"Maybe," he answered, circling an arm around her waist, "this plan is better because Newton isn't going to disturb us in here. I'd like very much to kiss you without the threat of being attacked from behind by a living tank."

"I probably shouldn't mention it, but doors are Newton's specialty."

"He wouldn't!"

"No, he wouldn't dare. Not the barn door. But I think he's capable of breaking even that door if he was determined enough. Fortunately, he has a sense of the limits to what I'll put up with. Sometimes."

"I hope so. From what I've seen, I'm not so sure."

Gently, he led her toward the far end of the barn. Broad streaks of yellow sunlight were streaming in through a high window. A ladder led to the loft above, where the fresh hay was stored.

He motioned to the ladder. "When was the last time you hid in your hayloft from intruders?"

"Too long to remember."

He started up the ladder. Her heart began fluttering as she watched him climb. The silence of the barn closed in when their voices ceased. The shadows seemed darker and the sunlight from the high window even brighter.

He lay on his stomach at the edge of the loft and looked down. "Are you too chicken to come up here with me?"

"I'm not afraid of you, if that's what you mean."

"I hope you're not. You've no reason to be afraid of me." He looked around. "Hey, it's nice up here. Sunny and warm." Clumsily, he threw aside his faded denim jacket and stretched luxuriously. He was wearing a white sweatshirt that was limp from many launderings.

Sunbeams were reflecting on the gold of the straw. Margie paused on the top rung of the ladder at the sight of him sprawled in the hay like a little boy. Straw was already in his hair.

He sat up and reached out his hand to help her up the last step. She felt the pressure of his hand tighten and then loosen again as he pulled her toward him, and she fell onto his chest, supported by the circle of his arms.

He held her close against him. She could feel his breathing. She was aware of her own breathing, finding the rhythm of his. And her own heartbeat finding the beat of his. They lay for a long time, saying nothing, just accepting each other. Accepting circumstances, however difficult those circumstances. Accepting the sun's warmth through the window and the soft straw under them. She sensed the moment when he was about to kiss her, because somehow it was exactly the right moment, when the acceptance was complete.

His lips moved over hers as gently as a morning breeze brushing flower petals, so slowly at first that her breath caught in anticipation. It was a long kiss, building to the intensity of heat, and it left them breathless.

He sighed shakily then and whispered, "I tried to resist you, Margie. I really did try."

"I know."

"You wouldn't let me."

"I didn't want you to resist me," she said softly. "I was afraid you'd know that I was . . . attracted to you, and I didn't know for sure what to do about that . . . I mean about you knowing. I've been awfully confused about you. When you looked at me, there was that something in your eyes that told me you wanted to stay. Yet you wouldn't . . . get too close to me, except when you kissed me by the fire."

"You saw right through me. I was trying to keep away, but my thoughts were of you. More than I wanted them to be. What you saw in my eyes when I looked at you was a man wanting to be close to you . . . and to touch you . . . and to kiss you . . . ."

His lips touched hers again. The sunbeams seemed to become part of his kiss. So did the blue frame of sky outside the window and the melodious song of a prairie bird in the highest branches of the giant cottonwood.

Margie closed her eyes and let the kiss flow through her, like the warmth of sun.

"It feels," Kyle whispered, as if he were inside her reading her thoughts and feeling the sensations of her body, "it feels so right."

"Yes," she breathed.

"It's warm up here," he said, and slid the shoulders of her jacket off her shoulders.

She wriggled out of the jacket and tossed it aside. He rose up on one elbow and looked at her in a way he never had before. "Margie, I wasn't prepared for you." He picked at the straw slowly. "I've tried for years to bury myself in my work, but then you . . . turned up one night on a snowy hillside. . . ." His voice trailed into the silence.

Gently, he drew her close and kissed her again, this time in a different way. It became a kiss between two people who knew each other and wanted each other, a kiss unhurried, slowly building to passion beyond anything either had ever known. She felt helplessness and power all at once, as though she had just lost herself and at the same time found herself. In her response to his kiss, she discovered a depth of longing known only to women who loved, who truly loved. And to her surprise, it was beyond any depth she'd ever reached before.

She could barely think, and yet thoughts came whirling at her from the vortex of Kyle's kiss. Love? How could she think the word? She barely knew him. How could she *not* think the word, when it was what she was experiencing full-blown and wild? Love. Whether she knew him or not, she loved Kyle!

And for the moment—at least for the moment—there was no doubt in her mind that he loved her. If not with his head, then with his heart. Everything about him said so, and everything within her said so, sang so, in an age-old melody that seemed hauntingly familiar, even though Margie knew she'd never heard it.

Love . . . within the enchantment of a kiss.

"Margie . . ." he uttered with his breath, not his voice.

She whispered back, "I know . . . yes . . . I know . . . I want . . . you, too. . . ."

"Honey . . ." he breathed between fluttery kisses, "are you sure?"

Margie gazed at him. A mist of sunlight from the high loft window filtered down on his hair and his face and the yellow-gold straw on which he was lying. A haze of light, blurred at the edges of the reality that was Kyle and this moment in time. A haze of light softening his features, blending in the softness of his eyes as he looked at her and whispered her name again.

"Yes," she answered from deep inside her heart, brushing her hand lightly over his chest. "Yes, I'm sure. . . ."

Gently he reached out to touch her face with his fingertips. "If we, uh . . ." His touch was like velvet fire on her cheek. "I won't be able to stop. . . ."

"I won't want you to stop."

His misty smile came as softly and as sensually as his touch. For a moment he closed his eyes and let his fingertips slide from her cheeks to her throat, moving under the collar of her shirt and over the bare skin of her shoulder.

Margie closed her eyes and allowed the shower of sensations to rain over her. His hands were gentle, caressing, along her throat, her breasts; his lips following the path of his fingers; his breath becoming hers.

New awareness—intense and exquisite awareness of his body—absorbed her senses. Softness of his chest hair against warm skin as her hand pushed up his sweatshirt. Hardness of the muscles of his shoulders and his chest. Fiery pressure of the lusty response of his loins against the softness of her abdomen.

Lips on her lips and on her breasts. Warmth of the sunlight on her bare skin. Heat of his breath.

So many words had been said this morning. Trust had been built solidly between them. There was no longer any need for words. Kyle tugged his boots off, then hers, threw off his sweatshirt and slid her already unbuttoned shirt down over her shoulders. His hands moved over the lace of her bra, releasing the hook, and holding her breasts, he bent to kiss her. With wild abandon, she moved her fingers through his thick dark hair.

Propped on one elbow, he made an awkward attempt to unbuckle his belt with his left hand. When her hand covered his, he turned and lay back to allow her to do it for him.

"Your hand is trembling," he said.

"My whole body is trembling. You do that to me."

His hand came over hers, strong and warm. "It's okay, Margie, don't be shy. Undress me."

"Your jeans are . . . tight."

"I'll help."

He kicked out of his clothes, lay back and closed his eyes. She indulged in the luxury of looking at him. His body was beautiful in its perfection: perfectly proportioned, strongly muscled, even more beautiful than she had imagined. There were lines of a not yet faded summer tan. The hair on his chest and legs, unfaded by sun like the hair on his arms, was darker than she'd thought it would be—darker than she remembered from the morning in his kitchen when he wore no shirt under his jacket.

In the grip of his own virile fever, he could not lie still. While she luxuriated in the beauty of him, he reached up to caress her face. His other hand found her belt buckle. "Come to me, Margie."

Within seconds he was tossing aside denim and lace and pulling her warm, naked body to his, cradling her in his arms.

He moaned with pleasure. "Ah . . . you feel so good."

"So do you."

His hands began to caress her, over her shoulders, her back, her hips. The caressing became exploring, gradually firmer, bolder, until she could not lie still.

With a great heave of his chest Kyle slid his body from beneath her. Margie wasn't sure how he did it so easily and without ceasing the gentle stroking of his hands. He moved with a kind of hypnotic rhythm, like waves, soft and hard at the same time. In the spell of rapture, he claimed his power over her.

Eyes shining in the sunlight, he gazed down at her. "You're beautiful. . . ." His lips sought hers in a long, deep kiss. Trying to hold on to the earth, to reality, was impossible for her. Her fingers slid helplessly from his neck; her arms fell limply at her sides. Her thighs trembled in anticipation of him.

She felt his lips move over her breasts once again, then down the length of her body, slowly, boldly, claiming possession of all of her. Magnificent and intolerable sensations. Margie heard herself cry his name.

Her cry caused a shudder of emotion to move through his body. She felt it and clung to him and heard her name whispered as if it came rushing from the crest of a wild wave.

"Margie . . . honey. I've waited so long for you . . . I can't wait now. . . ."

"Don't wait!"

His warmth became fire. And the fire shot through her as he moved over her and he gave to her the strength of his body and the strength of his love. The heat—his heat—rushed through her blood, consuming her. Heat borne on the moving flames of his kisses seared her eyes, her throat, her neck. He kissed her closed eyes softly, hotly. . . .

She opened her eyes in response to the pulse of his body on hers, gentle thrusts of passion becoming bold, becoming free, laying claim to the needs in her, asserting the immoderate, unsated need in him. His eyes met hers. She saw in them a glow of joy that caused her heart to surge and made her smile, mistily, dreamily. He smiled back, a soft, deep-reaching, intimate smile—gifts of sharing.

His deep breathing soared and rose in his chest. Ocean waves were his breaths. Ocean waves were the swelling rhythms of his body over her, against her, leading her, urging her toward wild crests. With him.

Margie let go of the world, of everything but Kyle, as a spasm of surrender overtook him, conquered him and finally left him free.

IN THE LENGTHENING SHADOWS of silence she stirred, groaning lowly. "Kyle?"

"Hmm?"

"You're very heavy."

"Oh, damn, I'm sorry. I was unconscious."

"I know."

He seemed disoriented as he lifted his body from hers. When the cool air replaced his warmth, she shivered, wanting the warmth back again. Already.

"I didn't realize all my weight was on you. You must be squashed."

"I must be."

He studied her. "Why are you smiling, Margie? I weigh two hundred pounds, and you must weigh barely over a hundred. How long... was I...?"

"I don't know. A long time. But you didn't hurt me. If you had, I'd have said so before. Did you fall asleep?"

"I don't know." He lay his head back and stared at the beamed ceiling of the loft. "There were fireworks. Really! I didn't know making love could be like that. It was as if...as if when my body let go, a tremendous dam broke and I was flooded with every feeling I've ever had. Emotionally, I couldn't quite handle it. There was you, and then the fireworks, and then everything went sort of blank."

She felt for his hand and held it in hers. Gently, she said, "There's so much pent-up inside you, Kyle. Something in you must want very much to..." Her voice dropped into silence.

"To what?"

"To be free."

His eyes closed. After a long pause of silence with shadows of a small cloud moving across the frame of the upper window, he answered, "You can't know how much I want to be free."

Margie swallowed. Tears formed in her eyes. She understood so little—except his frustration and his pain—about what had gone so terribly wrong in his life, or why.

Squeezing her hand with affection, he turned toward her and propped himself on his elbow, gazing over at her. "Are you okay, honey?"

"Yes, of course. I told you I wasn't really squashed."

"I don't mean that. I mean, we got so carried away...with passion that we didn't think...about risk."

She remembered that Kyle had asked her the same thing before. He'd had the presence of mind, out of concern for her, to ask. She'd understood and answered, but it had been so slight an answer—a tiny nod—that he was asking now, again. She, too, had heartbreaks she didn't want to talk about. But now she had to; he had asked.

"I can't...have children," she answered softly. "Maybe that's one reason I haven't married. Men want families, you know."

He frowned. "Are you sure?"

"Yes. Absolutely sure."

"I mean, are you sure all men want families?"

"They want to carry on the genes."

His crooked smile came slowly. "Not all men feel they have to have kids."

She studied him. "You don't have kids, do you?"

"No."

"Didn't you want them?"

"Yeah, when I was younger. It didn't happen. I don't think about it anymore."

"Your wife . . . ?" Margie's question dissolved into air, unasked.

But Kyle attempted to answer. "My wife had a history of psychological disorders. She wouldn't have been a good mother. Her psychological history is also the reason I haven't been able to get a divorce during these five years since she left me. Legally I can't get out from under this sham of a marriage until seven years have gone by. The whole thing is just damned complicated."

Margie asked, "She was a licensed pilot?"

"We both were. Her problems had nothing to do with her ability to fly. She was just . . . she had an unpredictable personality."

"Do you still fly?"

"No. I've lost interest."

"You really think she disappeared on purpose?"

"I don't know what else to think. Nothing else makes any sense."

Margie slid a little nearer to him. They were lying on their clothes now as protection from the straw. "If your wife is alive, might not Brockmeier find her?"

"He might. Someone might. Maybe my detective."

"You've hired a detective?"

"I want to find her, Margie. I don't give a damn about the money. It's not worth all this. The policy was Claire's idea in the first place. She wanted it because we were both pilots."

Margie realized this was still so painful for him. He wasn't over Claire yet. Perhaps he never would be.

"You've been through hell, haven't you, Kyle? These years of not knowing. It must be awful!"

"I won't pretend it hasn't been hell. The uncertainty is the worst part. I always feel as if I'm running from something, but running doesn't do any good. And waiting for something without knowing what." He closed his eyes, then opened them again and reached out to brush her blond hair away from her eyes. "I wish you weren't burdened with any of this."

"It's all so unfair to *you*. Look what it's done to your life. And that awful man investigating everything you do."

"I'll survive, honey. I always have."

"Sometimes your frustration really shows, though. I've seen it in your eyes and in your trigger temper."

"Guilty as charged."

She sighed, allowing her hand to leave his and travel the distance of his arm to his shoulder, where she began slowly to exert pressure with her fingertips along his collarbone. "I can feel the tension in your muscles. When was the last time you completely relaxed?"

"I wouldn't know."

"I think what you need is a good massage. Why not just turn over and close your eyes and let me massage your shoulders until you relax?"

He gazed at her. "Are you serious? You'd do that for me?"

"Why do you act so surprised? Of course I will."

Margie was deeply touched and a little saddened to see his reaction of surprise that she—that someone—would want to baby him a little, take care of him, as though he were completely unused to it. It told her a lot about him and the way he had lived for the past few years.

She urged him over onto his stomach. He lay on his sweatshirt, arms above his head, and closed his eyes. Starting at his neck, Margie massaged him firmly, using her fingertips and the heels of her hands. The broad expanse of his back was a reminder of Kyle's size. He didn't give the impression of being as big as he was, probably because he was so perfectly proportioned. But lying next to him and now straddling his hips and leaning over him, Margie was marveling once again at the beauty of him.

He moaned with pleasure. "You have the touch of an angel."

"Angels seem so . . . sort of feathery. I wish I were stronger."

"No complaints here." His voice was muffled as if he were half-asleep. "Actually, I was just thinking that your hands are pretty strong."

"You're tense, Kyle, you really are. I'm glad we took today for us. We need today. I can feel you relaxing."

"I can feel it, too. I may fall asleep...."

"Sleep, then." Her hands moved in tight circles along his shoulder blades to the small of his back. Except for occasional breaths expressing his pleasure, he lay in silence, allowing her spell to pull him under.

At length he stirred. "Honey, aren't you cold?"

"Are you?"

"No, not with you all warm and naked sitting on me. But it isn't all that warm in here now."

"Why are you worrying about that? You're supposed to be falling asleep."

"I don't want you to be cold."

"All right. There are blankets downstairs. I'll get them and be right back."

In the main part of the small barn, she took saddle blankets from a shelf, blankets that hadn't been used since her father died, and shaking the dust from them, examined them. They were soft and passably clean.

A snorting sound came from outside the door. Newton was still out there. Margie smiled. One thing about Newton—he was persistent and not easily distracted once he was involved in his bodyguard job.

Kyle was asleep by the time she returned to the loft. Throwing one of the blankets over her shoulders, she stood for some moments looking down at him, at his body, at the way his hands curled, relaxed in sleep. At his thick hair, falling over his forehead. At the shadow of his eyelashes on his arm in the gauzy slant of sunshine that beamed down from the window. Her heart filled to bursting with emotion—unfamiliar emotion that she could identify only as love. *I really do love him*, the voice of her heart was saying.

Quietly, not wanting to wake him, Margie lay down beside him, snuggling her body next to his, pulling the blanket over them both. Kyle stirred, rolled onto his side with a little groan of pleasure and drew her into his arms. Wrapping himself around her, he held her tightly.

Margie closed her eyes, feeling a pleasure she hadn't felt ever before, ever in her life. So this was what love was like—this wanting, this belonging next to someone. *He needs me*, she thought as sunbeams danced through the lavender shadows and the sound of Kyle's soft, even breathing blended with her own.

It was only as she was drifting into a dream state that something startled her. At first, she wasn't sure what it was, but slowly it became evident that what had frightened her was not something external; it was something inside her.

If after five years there had been no sign of Kyle's wife, what could happen now to change that? Apparently the insurance company hadn't given up trying, nor had Kyle. What did he feel when he thought of finding his wife? Margie wondered. What did he feel when he thought of long ago moments with her?

He sighed softly in his sleep. Protectively, she touched his forehead lightly with her fingers. He had forgotten until today what it was like to be pampered with a caring touch. But surely he must have known tenderness— once.

9

KYLE STIRRED.

As gentle strokes like the feel of velvet grazed his temple, he reached up sleepily, took her hand in his and kissed her fingertips softly—so softly that tiny shivers trembled through her body.

She whispered, "Did I wake you?"

"I don't think so."

"I'm sorry if I did."

"No, you didn't. Honey, something is bothering me. Something you said." He shifted with a breathy grunt, but his fingers were still caressing her cheek. "Could Wayne Brockmeier hurt you?"

Margie winced. "You're remembering my remark about not liking him probing into my past?"

"Yeah." His hand moved to her arm, caressing.

She looked away, at the sunlight on straw below the window.

"Damn him!" he cursed. "It's my fault, though. If I hadn't—"

"It's not your fault." Her gaze came back to him. "I can understand why you didn't want to talk about your past, Kyle. I understand about trying to carry on living as though the past never . . . happened."

He smiled softly. "You're the last person I'd have associated with a secret past. Your life, your surroundings, this town . . ."

"I know. People who live in towns like Rosewood rarely have very private lives. Everything is everybody's business." She lowered her head. "I guess that detective will tell you about me if I don't."

"You don't have to tell me anything."

She leaned back against a bale of hay, knees up, the blanket draped carelessly over her. "Brockmeier believes that you and I had secret trysts in Europe just because we happened to be there at the same time. I was in southern France. Were you ever in France?"

"Yeah, for a few days. But that's stretching reason to ridiculous extremes, even for him."

"He already knows where you were. Where I was. Maybe we were at the same place at the same time."

"I strongly doubt it. Too coincidental."

Margie nodded. "But he'll try to connect it anyway."

Kyle already understood. The past that Margie guarded had to do not with Rosewood but with France.

She read his thoughts. "Long ago and far away. I was so much younger then."

"And probably in love."

"Yes."

His voice was soft. "It happens."

"I was very foolish."

"Weren't we all."

"He was very handsome and very rich, and spoiled...."

Kyle pushed himself up into a sitting position and moved close to her, resting his hand on her thigh. "You don't have to tell me. It's your—"

She interrupted. "I'd rather you heard it from me than from him."

"The way you had to hear about me."

"I didn't mean—"

"I know you didn't. But it was a hell of a way to have to learn about me, and half lies at that. But Brockmeier may never talk to me about you."

"Do you really believe that?"

"No. I never know what he'll do."

Margie fell into a short silence before she said in a small voice, "I know what you're thinking. That I went to France and fell in love with a Frenchman and probably found out he was married and I came home with a broken heart."

"Is that how it was?"

"No."

Margie waited for the awful, sinking emptiness to enter her heart the way it always did when she thought back to that year in France. But strangely, it didn't come. She'd never talked to a living soul, at least not a soul in the United States, about any of it; this was the first time. And the memory came now with more detachment than ever before, almost as if it had happened to someone else. Long ago.

"It was horrible, Kyle. Not just a sour love affair. It was very... horrible the way it turned out. I was there visiting a friend I'd gone to the university with, and his family and her family were friends. We met the very first day I arrived. He spoke English and at first I was so helpless in French. We really did love each other... I know I loved *him*... and I loved the summer and the French Riviera and the lakes and horseback riding and the art museums. It was all like a dream to a girl from rural Nebraska. You can imagine." She paused and looked at him, and he merely nodded and squeezed her hand.

"I was so much in love I wasn't devastated to learn I was pregnant. Troi was happy. He wanted the baby, and I naturally supposed we'd marry, although it frightened me some to think of living in France for the rest of my life. I was so different from all of them and I knew I could never fit in, never become one of Troi's kind of people. Not only were they French, they were wealthy and... extravagant. But I assumed we'd marry since we were going to be parents, and we loved each other. Too late I learned he was betrothed—that's the word they used—'betrothed' to another woman, a longtime arrangement in keeping with his social status. Neither his family nor Troi had any intention of not going through with that marriage. He wanted his baby, though. I have reason to believe that he intended to get the baby away from me if I refused to stay in France like he wanted."

It felt so strange saying it, saying all of it out loud to another human being. To Kyle. Margie's voice became softer and softer as she talked, until he could barely hear her.

He could feel her pain. Words wouldn't help, but his arm around her shoulder, comforting, did help. She tried to smile her gratitude for the protective warmth of him.

He had shown no sign of shock over her story, no indication that he felt anything but understanding. Kyle was experienced in life, she thought. More than most people. He wasn't a man to judge others. And he had, after all, been honest with her about his own past when he finally opened up.

"You said 'reason to believe.' What happened, Margie?"

Her answer came on the sighs of a whisper. "I had a daughter. It was a difficult birth, and I was told I couldn't bear any more children. Her name was Michelle and she was beautiful. I knew I couldn't bring her back to Rosewood and raise her here. You can see why I couldn't. I was trying desperately to decide what to do, and my friends were urging me to stay in France . . . and then one day I was driving back to Toulouse from Paris with my friend Isobel and the baby, and we were hit by another car and Michelle was killed instantly. I had a concussion and Isobel was uninjured. Troi blamed me because I was driving, but I couldn't have prevented the accident because we were hit from behind. The baby was in the back seat. . . ."

She sighed deeply, sadly. "Troi was no comfort. He was only into his own pain. His family was planning his wedding and he didn't want to see me anymore."

Kyle's arm tightened around her and he sat in silence, holding her.

At length he said huskily, "I'm sorry. . . ."

Margie leaned into him. "I'd hate for people here to know."

"They won't if I can help it. I think I'd better have a talk with my attorney. Make a few threats. Until I'm officially accused of anything, I have the rights of any other citizen, and this thing with the insurance company has gotten out of hand."

"You don't seem worried about being accused of murder, Kyle. You just slough that off."

"I'm not worried about it because there wasn't any murder."

"Can they get you on circumstantial evidence for conspiracy?"

"No. If they could, they would have by now. There's just nothing, Margie. Claire vanished. I don't know how she did it and neither does anybody else."

"You're still hoping they'll find her."

"Hell, yes. And end this nightmare. I want to get on with my life."

With a heavy sigh, he began to caress the back of her neck. "I admire the way you've put your past behind you."

"I had no choice."

"You like living here, don't you?"

"Yes. I love this valley. I belong here. When I was a kid I always dreamed of seeing the world. The grass seemed always greener in the exotic-sounding places—you know. But that isn't true. Our grass is as green as anywhere."

"I think so, too."

She smiled. "Oh, how tongues would wag over your situation, Kyle, if people knew. And over my secret, if people knew."

"And over us together. That they'll know soon enough."

"That I really don't mind."

"Neither do I. Not anymore. I wouldn't let myself think about how much I wanted to be with you. Now I can admit it, to myself and to you."

"It doesn't matter to you that I've...what I've told you about me?"

This question clearly stunned him. "Why the hell would it matter to me? Except that I'm sorry you've had so much pain. I can see the death of your daughter is too painful for you to talk about. Maybe it always will be."

"Maybe."

"If you ever do want to talk about it, though, I'm here. Okay?"

She nodded. What a strange feeling it was not to be alone. To have someone to talk to who cared. She wondered if it was that way for him too—a need fulfilled to be able to talk openly to her of a life so full of tragedy.

With eyes full of love, she looked at him. He leaned close and kissed her—a tender kiss, a loving kiss. High branches outside the window quivered in a breeze and cast moving shadows over his body. He sat naked beside her, not having bothered to cover himself. Shadows fluttering in gold sheaves of sunlight slanted down on him, and when Margie turned to him now, she thought, *he is beauty.*

The sharing, the closeness, magnified the need. The loving kiss was replaced by a hungry one.

"I want you," he said.

He drew aside the blanket that covered her and spread it out for her to lie on. Pulling her gently down onto it, he lay beside her, smoothing his hands over her body. She reached up to him and kissed him. They began to move in rhythm to the responding needs of their bodies as the kiss caught them on its crest and carried them toward still undiscovered passions.

"Margie, touch me...."

He guided her hand to his chest and over his abdomen, then stopped, waiting for her.

She responded with her touch, with gentle pressure of her hand, gentle warmth of her caressing fingers.

He exhaled a heavy, shaky breath. "You feel so good."

"So do you."

"I like it when you do that."

"And this?"

"Umm..." His eyes closed.

She felt no chill without the blanket. Heat was in him, and in her, and flaming. She moved the length of her body against his as she abandoned every thought but the pure, soaring joy of giving pleasure to him.

He began to moan. "Wait, my love…wait for me…I want to touch you…I want…" His voice and breath became one.

His hands came trembling to her breasts, rippling over her skin like hot liquid fire. Over her stomach, her abdomen, her hips, stroking the softness of her, he sought the essence of her…finding the need in her.

"You want me, too," he whispered.

"Yes…"

His voice was husky. "Let me…know you. I want to know all of you. I want you to know all of me."

Trembling, she accepted the exploration of his lips. Trembling, she accepted his body joining hers. She cried out his name in a rush of exploding emotion—accepting. Accepting completely. Giving completely. And from somewhere in the vortex of love, she heard the sound of her own name on his exhaling breath as the tremors of release overtook him.

"Margie…I love you…"

SPRING BURST into being and surrounded them. In the coming days, the earth seemed to forget completely that there had ever been a layer of snow or a crust of frost over its surface. The first impatient leaf buds fuzzed the trees, and spears of green colored the face of the landscape. Wildflowers began to appear, almost shyly, on the sunny slopes just above the stream.

It was their spring. Days to walk together in the yellow sunlight. Evenings to listen to dove calls and watch the slowly rising moon. Nights to lie together in Margie's bedroom. Dewy mornings to wake in each other's arms.

For a week, they didn't discuss Kyle's past again . . . or hers. They lived the beauty of the present, savoring every moment together, and each moment lived for itself.

Sometimes a shadow would blow over the sun and doubts would come to Margie. What, she wondered, did Claire Sanders look like? What sort of woman was she? They must have loved each other once. He believed she'd left him for another man. She'd chosen a pretty bizarre way to leave her husband, if in fact that's what had happened. What would his feelings be about his wife if she were found?

KYLE FELT THE SHADOWS, too. He knew Brockmeier had left town, no doubt for Florida. The rumors, then, were substantial enough to warrant an investigation there. Kyle's own hired detective thought so, and obviously Brockmeier did, too. It was the first trace of encouragement in years, but still not enough for him to build real hope on. A thousand times he'd asked himself why Claire would have chosen to put him through such hell. He hadn't come to terms with her betrayal and probably never would.

Margie made a difference, a tremendous difference. She made him remember what it was to look forward to tomorrow. What it was to be loved, and to love. Margie needed him in all the ways a woman needed a man. And he . . . he needed the love of a woman. Kyle mentioned nothing to Margie about the Florida rumor. It was, after all, no more than a rumor. The burden of what it meant was his to contemplate, not hers.

Kyle and Newton made up. An offering of a sweet potato and a sack of jelly beans had done the trick. The pig accepted the fact that the man was going to be around the house whether he liked it or not, and this Newton could tolerate if the prizes continued coming. They did. After a doubtful beginning, the two were forming a kind of involuntary friendship.

AT THE END of the second week, Margie's job called her out of town. She had agreed to do auctions in three towns in the county, which meant three days away from home.

Dick Campbell always fed her animals when she was out of town, an arrangement that was fine with Angel, who was happy as long as she could romp in the meadows and chase frogs along the stream. When no one was in the house, Angel slept in the barn, which Margie never locked.

Pig Newton was the problem. He had decided Dick Campbell had no business snooping around their property, and it had almost reached a point at which Dick refused to come. He, along with everybody else, was terrified he might anger Newton, the pig's reputation for viciousness being what it was during his career as a sheriff's deputy. Margie always worried about someone getting hurt when Newton was guarding her property.

When she expressed her concerns to Kyle, he came up with an immediate solution.

"Newton can stay with me."

Standing by his truck in the morning cool, Margie squinted up at him. "Are you sure you want Newton at your house?"

He looked over at the pig, who was rooting around the flower beds by the front porch, paying no attention to the humans. "Newton and I have developed a sort of mutual understanding. He didn't even snort at me when I was shaving in your bathroom this morning. In fact, he ate three scoops of shaving cream."

"You gave him shaving cream?"

"He was fascinated by the foam—thought it was whipping cream, I suppose, and insisted on tasting it. You know how Newton can insist. So I squirted it all over his nose and he stood in front of the mirror admiring himself for a good minute before he licked it off and wanted more." Kyle chuckled. "Would he get in my pickup?"

"Sure. He'll love going with you. I'll get his ramp."

Minutes later Newton was standing in the bed of the truck, looking over the gate and happily chewing on an entire package of peppermint gum that Kyle had used as a bribe. Excited, he began snorting loudly.

"Okay, we're going," Kyle said. "Just take it easy!"

He held Margie tightly against his chest and kissed her goodbye. "Till you get back . . ." he whispered.

She stood in her yard and waved at them as the pickup bounced over the narrow dirt road that led to her gate and down the road a mile to his.

"Behave while I'm gone, Newton," she breathed. "Please behave. . . ."

THINGS WENT SMOOTHLY for two days. The weather was warming and Pig Newton was content to spend most of his days snoozing on the soft new grass in the shade of the porch eaves. He took time from this major activity to explore his new surroundings. Angel showed up regularly, running back and forth between their houses, but Newton seemed to understand that going to all the inconvenience of hiking home would be a waste of energy and time, because his lady was not there.

The third morning it was raining. Before Kyle left for work, he propped open the door of the back screen porch so that the animals would have shelter from the drizzly skies. It was a large porch off the kitchen on which Kyle stored raincoats and boots and various supplies.

The gray skies may have been an omen; the day was a bad one for Kyle from beginning to end. He discovered he'd misplaced an important file in his move, then lost a contract when his client phoned to say a building had been canceled because of financial problems. And in the afternoon he received a phone call from his attorney with news from his private detective, John Dillon, that all he'd found so far in Miami was Wayne Brockmeier, who had learned who Dillon was and had cornered him in a restaurant to ask a lot of questions.

Kyle began calculating in his head how much John Dillon and the attorney were costing him, and depression bore down on him. If only he could just drop the whole nightmare—all of it. Just close his eyes and have it gone. If only he could even release it in his mind, stop pursuing it and just accept the fact that Claire was gone and, as far as he was concerned, might as well be dead.

He was unable to let go of it; he had to know. She may have gone off alone and somehow met with foul play. She may have suffered psychological problems, even lost her memory. Anything was possible. Whatever else had come between them, if she was alive she was still his wife.

After the phone call from Omaha he tried to work, but his brain was sluggish. Thoughts of Margie kept rushing to the forefront of his mind, sweet thoughts that he couldn't help but try to hold on to. Margie would be home tomorrow morning. It was useless trying to finish the work he had set out for himself this late afternoon. He needed to relax and try to forget the day; he was exhausted. At five o'clock he closed up his office and headed home, only to discover when he got there that his problems had only begun. Nothing could have prepared him for the sight that met his eyes.

Beer cans, punctured and empty, were scattered all over the back lawn and the porch steps and the porch. Newton was sprawled out on the top step, his rump hanging off the side and a huge smile on his face.

Kyle swore a stream of oaths as he jumped out of his pickup, ignoring the greeting of his dog, who was leaping happily at his legs.

Sticky beer was everywhere; it stuck to his boots as he climbed the steps. Only now, too late, did he remember the case of beer he'd stored on his back porch.

Incredulously, he stared at the pig, who rolled his big head sideways and looked up at Kyle blinking stupidly. "Damn you, Newton! I ought to kill you for this! Margie is going to kill us both."

Trying to move the pink hulk was useless. Kyle muttered oaths at him, calling him an inebriated sot, while he tried to wash the floor clean with a bucket of water. With the rush of water on him, Newton raised his head, squealed weakly and wriggled his nose at the man. The second bucket brought more protest; Newton oinked and struggled to his feet.

Wobbling, he staggered over the porch around Kyle's feet, nearly tripping him time and again while Kyle tried to sweep out the water.

"I'm not even gonna count these cans," Kyle growled aloud. "But it looks like you've just done away with a whole damn case of beer. And you're supposed to be on the wagon. All Margie's efforts at rehabilitation..."

The pig was feeling especially friendly and kept leaning into the man's legs, smiling. Kyle slipped on the slick boards and nearly fell for the third time. He swore aloud, made a few more threats and then scratched his head in utter frustration. "I can't believe it! Here I am talking to a drunk pig!" Newton looked up at him with affection in his tiny, glazed eyes.

"The hell with it!" Kyle howled, throwing down the broom. "This mess can wait until I've had a drink myself. Why should you be the only one drinking?"

He stomped into the house, kicking off his boots inside the kitchen door. Slamming around, he pulled a bottle from the cabinet, found a glass and filled it half-full. One hearty swallow helped. He looked down. Newton had swaggered in with him and was standing at his side now, looking up with glassy eyes and the pasted-on grin and wriggling his snout in anticipation.

Kyle scowled at him in disgust. "You're already drunk as a swine. If you think you're gonna get any more..." He set down his glass. "All you're gonna get is kicked outside." He began to push the pig toward the door.

It wasn't an easy job getting Newton to the back porch again. By the time Kyle accomplished it, he was sweating profusely.

He choked back the rest of the liquor in his glass in record time, poured it full again and made his way into the living room, where he plopped onto the couch. Thunder sounded outside, a low rumble at first, and gradually it began to get louder. With the rainy skies it had been cool all day, but the night was turning very chilly. The house felt damp and cold and empty.

With kindling and logs that were stacked on the mantel, Kyle built a fire, got it blazing and sat back on the floor drinking and staring into the flames.

He knew Newton would sober up before Margie got back, but still he'd have to tell her what had happened. Hell, he'd have to get out there first thing in the morning and finish cleaning up the horrendous mess. He heard the dog at the back door and got up to feed him. Newton ignored his own dinner, sniffing at it with indifference, unable to walk in a straight line or even stand up for very long at a time.

King scampered off to the barn to keep an eye on the resident cats, Newton fell in a heap by the door and Kyle, not in the mood to fix any dinner for himself, settled down by the fire with his glass and drowned himself in self-pity. It had been a rotten day, and he felt a bone-weary kind of exhaustion overtake him.

He thought of Claire and he thought of Margie, and the thoughts of Margie brought with them a special warmth he couldn't remember ever experiencing before, ever in his life. Margie made him more determined than ever to shed the cloaked shadows of his past and start to live again. It was easy with Margie, because she made him feel so alive.

And he did the same for her, he knew. It felt fine—felt right—loving Margie, except for the shadows, the unanswered questions, the inescapable truth that he was married.

Later, when the fire started to burn down, he got up to throw on another log and realized he was very unsteady on his feet. Two lousy drinks and he was getting drunk. No, not drunk. Tired. He should have eaten something, he knew.

The fire warmed him. Its soft crackling was soothing, like a lullaby. Before another hour had passed, he had fallen into exhausted sleep.

THE SMELL OF SMOKE woke Newton. He raised his head and looked around, nose snuffling, instantly alert to danger. He rose shaking himself. His massive weight had thrown off most of the effects of the alcohol in the couple of hours that he'd been asleep. The German shepherd, King, bounded onto the porch, rain wet and barking furiously, jumping on the door. There was no sound whatever from within.

Only smoke and silence.

Newton grunted and squealed loudly, then louder still. King was jumping about frantically. But King did not possess the advantage of Newton's incredible strength. Not fifteen seconds had passed before the trained police pig had, with minimum effort, smashed the door to the floor.

The dog reeled back at the burst of smoke that came from inside. The house was filled with it. But, head bent downward, snorting, Newton entered like an invading army tank, making almost as much noise as one. King followed, choking, throwing his head about, as determined as the pig to find his master.

In the living room, Kyle lay unmoving, still on his stomach, head in his arms. A large log had rolled out of the fire and was sparking. The rug was smoldering, throwing a blanket of heavy smoke through the house.

King leaped on him, pulling at his shirt with his teeth and emitting small yelps. There was no response. Newton jammed his snout hard into the man's armpit. Kyle moaned with the pain and moved his arm and began to cough, then to choke.

Overcome by the effects of breathing smoke, he was aware of pain, aware of something terribly wrong. His head was spinning in black swirls. His chest felt as if it were bursting, and he couldn't seem to move.

Somehow it seemed important to try to move, but the effort was too great. He felt a fierce jab of pain in his armpit again and opened his eyes to the realization that something large and pink was assaulting him, hurting him like hell and forcing him awake. He didn't want to be awake. His eyes closed again and he welcomed the blackness. The pain in his chest was excruciating—so excruciating that he would not and could not move, yet he didn't have the strength to resist the painful pushing and shoving of some massive, incredibly strong force that was upon him and wouldn't let go of him.

Through his groggy, smoke-strangled consciousness came an urgent message that he could vaguely identify. Danger. A few feet in front of him the gray air was turning orange. Wild streaks of orange leaped toward the ceiling. *I have a fever*, he thought deliriously at first, and then, *fire!* This was not fever fire, this fire was real!

There were hideous sounds around him—the sucking, cracking sounds of flames, hideous squealing of some kind and barking. Kyle wasn't sure what he was hearing, except that the noise was almost deafening, and the thing that was shoving him hurt and he had to get away from it.

He couldn't . . . couldn't move, but the thing with the loud shrieks and squeals kept pushing. Trying to get to his feet, Kyle moaned and fell.

He couldn't stand, so he attempted to crawl. There was so much smoke he couldn't tell where to go, but the pushing thing wouldn't allow him that decision anyhow. It yanked and shoved while through the terror and confusion, King yelped incessantly.

The pain in his chest gripped Kyle so viciously that he lost awareness of everything else. Orange air gave way to gray, then black—great, hideous swirls of black, circling over him. Then there was only pain, and finally, only blackness.

10

THE ANNOUNCER on her car radio had just given the time—8:40 p.m. Late to be getting home. Still, tired as she was, Margie was glad she had driven back tonight instead of waiting until morning. It had been a long three days without Kyle. She'd kept busy with the auctions she had to do, but those two evenings alone were long and very dark. The weather was cold and rainy—those typical cold, rainy days that were a necessary part of spring in the midwest.

Almost mesmerized by sparkles of drizzling rain in her headlights, Margie's attention was diverted by a change she saw in the sky as she turned off onto the gravel road that wound down through a series of meadows toward the ranch houses. Smoke!

Fear gripped her. One of the houses or barns, either hers or Kyle's must be burning! With pounding heart and racing thoughts, Margie tried her best to curtail panic. It might be one of the smaller outbuildings or even a haystack.

No, the smoke was too black for burning hay. Definitely a building was on fire. It looked too close for her house; it must be on Kyle's ranch.

When she pushed her foot heavily on the gas pedal, the car began to spin in the slippery, wet sand; it was impossible to go any faster on this road. Breathing faster, feeling her hands grow weak, Margie could only swallow and try to control the car while she watched the smoke grow nearer with each passing second.

It was Kyle's house that was burning! Drawing nearer, she saw flames leaping from the roof. There were lights on in his barn and several vehicles around there, no doubt the trucks of neighbors who had seen the smoke and come to help. Surely Kyle was all right, she told herself with determination. Surely he got out of the house and was safe! And the animals, too! How could the fire have started? Lightning, perhaps? There may have been an electrical storm here. It was an old, wood-frame house, the kind that burns most easily.

Turning into his open gate and driving the final quarter mile to the house, Margie began to experience small whirls of fright. The fear began in the pit of her stomach and seemed to be whirring its way to her heart. "He's all right!" she said aloud, gripping the steering wheel until her knuckles were white.

Behind her, lights came into view, moving fast from the curve of the county road. Flashing lights. An ambulance! Her heart nearly stopped.

She was at the edge of the big yard now. Slamming off the headlights, she swung in next to a pickup truck. Two fire trucks were parked next to the house. The noise was hideous: the sounds of water sizzling and slashing at the fire, people shouting, the flames cracking and howling.

Margie frantically ran past several stunned people, not speaking to them, not caring who they were. Their identities didn't matter to her, although they were neighbors, close friends.

In the floodlights water sparkled as it splashed onto the roof from hoses. An eerie glow from the fire and the lights lay over everything. Human forms moved in and out of shadows, their voices carrying on the drizzly night air.

"Kyle! Kyle, where are you?"

Suddenly Angel was there, jumping on her, and seconds later Pig Newton was pushing his massive body against her leg. But she did not see Kyle.

A few people were gathered, some kneeling, forty yards or so from the house in a clearing off the drive. She closed her eyes in a small silent prayer and muttered Kyle's name again on a trembling voice, knowing, just knowing, that he was in trouble.

Rushing to the clearing with the dog and pig following like bouncing shadows behind her, Margie pushed her way past the women circled there. Kyle lay on the ground on his back, his head turned to one side, his hair over his forehead, the way he often slept. Someone had thrown a blanket over him to protect him from the chilly drizzle. He simply looked asleep.

Margie was almost too frightened to speak. Kneeling at his side, she managed to cry his name on a high half voice that sounded to her as if it belonged to someone else. Slowly she became aware of the presence of two neighbors, Janet Murray and Sharon Campbell, kneeling beside her.

"There's not a mark on him!" Janet told her. "He was lying unconscious just outside the back porch, barefoot and covered with sweat. He's suffering from smoke inhalation, we think, Margie. The men moved him out here farther from the house."

Something shrieked in Margie's brain: *smoke inhalation can kill people!* She bent over him, tugging at his arms and shoulders. "Kyle! Can you hear me?"

Taking a cue from her, King nudged him hard. Kyle moved slightly, but there was no way for them to tell whether it was an actual response to her or whether his limp body had been moved by the dog.

Sharon Campbell leaned forward. "We can't figure out how he managed to get out of the house or when he lost consciousness. Is he still breathing?"

"Only with difficulty. . ." Margie answered in a weak, shaking voice as she slid her hand under the blanket to feel his chest. At first she felt nothing, then a small, jerky rise of breath.

Through a blur of darkness and the smell of smoke and shadows of flames on the trees and the fear that was tearing at her, Margie noticed flashes of light near the house. A flash camera. Someone must be taking flash pictures of the fire, but she couldn't imagine which of their neighbors would bring a camera to a fire. The flashes were getting closer; whoever had the camera was walking to where Kyle was lying, but it was impossible to identify the photographer in the dark.

In a moment the pictures no longer mattered because the ambulance lights were flashing in the yard and two paramedics were being directed toward the circle where Kyle lay. They rushed in with a stretcher and a medical bag, trying to keep out of the way of Newton, who somehow sensed their importance in all this and ran forward grunting, a self-appointed reception committee.

Rising from Kyle's side to give the medics room to work, Margie stood back, trying to hold King out of the way. The shepherd was overwrought and ready to protect his master from these strangers who dared touch him.

One of the men put a stethoscope to Kyle's chest. In the hush of silence that fell over the small group, only a low pig's grunt could be heard. Seconds later an oxygen mask was secured to the victim's face and the medics were checking his vital signs with a sense of urgency.

Desperately afraid for his life, Margie wanted more than anything on earth to stay with Kyle until he reached the hospital. But she would be in the way of the paramedics who needed to minister lifesaving attention to him.

As the paramedics were preparing to lift him onto the stretcher, a flashbulb burst forth. In the intense rush to get Kyle to a hospital, the others ignored the cameraman, but Margie realized those flashes had been on Kyle since the ambulance came.

She saw the man with the camera then and recognized him. Bill Stoddard was a reporter for the daily paper; he'd moved to Rosewood less than a year ago. His camera was aimed at Kyle, who lay on the gurney with an oxygen mask held over his face.

"Don't!" Margie protested.

The reporter stared at her blankly for a second or two before he flashed a final picture.

The anger that washed over her quickly gave way to greater concerns.

Urgency prevailed. The paramedics hadn't wasted a second. Their driver was starting the engine even before the doors were closed. Margie could do nothing but watch the ambulance pull out and disappear behind the trees that lined the lane to the gate.

Helplessly, she turned back. The fire fighters were still throwing water on the house, but flames were no longer visible; the fire was being contained.

"Why'd you yell at me?" Bill Stoddard approached her.

A blank stare met his. "What?"

"When I was taking pictures of Kyle Sanders you yelled at me to stop. Why?"

She frowned and pulled her shirt collar higher over her neck. "Would you like somebody to take a lot of pictures of you when you're unconscious?"

"Never thought about it. Hell—" the man made a sweeping gesture with his right hand "—this is *news!*"

"What do you do, follow fire trucks?"

"I investigate fires, yeah. What other excitement ever goes on around here?" He checked a lever on his camera. "Did the paramedics say why he was unconscious? Smoke inhalation?"

"They didn't stop to explain anything. They were in a hurry. What do you plan to do with those pictures?"

"Write a story about this fire and the fire casualty. What else would I do with it? This guy Sanders, I know him from somewhere, I could swear I do."

She had knelt down and was petting King, trying with the sure strokes of her hand to reassure Kyle's faithful pet that everything was all right.

The reporter stood over her. "One of the paramedics said something about inserting a trachea tube so Sanders could breathe."

A shiver passed through her. "I didn't hear anything like that."

"I did." Bill Stoddard shielded his camera from the rain with his jacket and looked back at the fire, which was now only smoldering. "I'm going to the hospital and find out whether the guy is going to survive or not. I covered a fire in Omaha where a guy died of heart failure from smoke inhalation. Young guy, too. Younger than Kyle Sanders."

With clenched fists, Margie rose. "Go chase your ambulance," she said in the calmest voice she was able to muster. Then, watching him disappear into the darkness of the long drive, she stood with her heart thudding. She'd realized that Kyle was having difficulty breathing. Obviously, the paramedic had seen at once that he was in serious trouble.

She closed her eyes. "Please, God . . ." she muttered aloud into a rush of wet wind. "Please . . ."

Margie turned back to her car, leading King, with Angel and Newton following behind. The animals sensed something terribly wrong—not just the fire but something more. They'd seen Kyle being carried away.

She opened the car door and the animals jumped in, the shepherds in the front, Newton in the back seat. "I have to go to the hospital," she said to them. "I'm going to get you guys settled down and then I have to go."

Once they were home, they seemed to calm down some, grateful to be warm and out of the rain. Margie hurried to change out of her wet clothes into dry jeans and a lavender sweatshirt, making herself take five minutes to blow-dry her hair.

When she left, the dogs had settled onto the living-room rug, but Newton restlessly followed her across the house to the back door. He rubbed against her leg and snorted softly.

"What is it, Newton?" she asked, reaching down to pet his nose. "What do you know about that fire?" Margie fought down panic. All she could think about was that Kyle was fighting this moment for his life.

TO HER SURPRISE and great relief, Bill Stoddard, the reporter, was not at the hospital. Her first inquiries at the desk were useless. There was no information, the nurse said. But after waiting half an hour, with insistent questions every five minutes, Margie was finally told that after two hours in emergency, Kyle had just been moved to a room in the respiratory unit.

"What is his condition?" she asked the nurse at the desk.

"I don't have that information."

Margie frowned and leaned across the counter. "But he was in the emergency room for so long. How serious . . . ?"

The nurse smiled reassuringly. "There are tests and X rays to do in emergency to determine what chemicals are in the blood and the condition of his lungs. If he had breathed a lot of toxic fumes, he'd be in intensive care right now instead of the respiratory ward. Since they're not taking him to I.C.U., we can assume he's all right."

A tremendous pressure lifted from her heart. Margie sighed shakily. "Oh, thank God! Can I see him?"

"It's long past visiting hours."

"Just for a minute? I wouldn't stay. I just want to see for myself that he's all right."

The nurse's eyes were soft and her manner gentle. She wanted to help, Margie knew. It probably wasn't fair to insist she break the rules, but rules didn't matter. Nothing mattered but Kyle and knowing he was going to recover.

The nurse was shuffling papers. "Let me check with a doctor." She rose and left the desk, disappearing through a door into the main corridor of the hospital.

Margie felt a chill as she looked around the empty room in the silence of the late hour. The smell of the hospital, the silence, save for voices far away down the hall and the sound of a gurney being rolled over hard linoleum floors, made the place eerie and depressing.

In a few minutes the nurse returned. "I just spoke with a doctor. He said he'd have spoken with you himself, but there's a baby waiting to be delivered. I'm to tell you that the patient is still experiencing considerable discomfort, but he should be able to get some rest tonight—"

"He's conscious?"

"Yes. But he's had a rough time of it this past couple of hours. The best thing for him is to rest now. He's been given medication, which will ease the discomfort some."

"Does all this mean I can't see him?"

The nurse moved behind the counter once again to answer the blinking phone light. "The doctor didn't say specifically that you couldn't. I suppose if you didn't disturb him . . ."

"Oh, I wouldn't! I wouldn't. I'd just look in on him."

The woman pushed the phone button and held her hand over the receiver. "Well, I didn't see you. I can't see every little thing that goes on around here."

"Thanks," Margie breathed. "Where is the—"

"One thirty-one." She pushed a button on the phone. "Rosewood Memorial Hospital . . ."

The woman's voice faded as Margie hurried down the wide corridor. Her palms were sweating; the fear had not completely subsided in spite of the reassurances she had just received.

Even at this hour of night, there were lights on in the room. A nurse was leaning over one of the beds; in the other two, both occupied, patients were sleeping quietly. Margie stood in the doorway for several seconds, until the nurse straightened and turned toward her. The patient was visible then from the doorway.

Kyle was lying on his back, eyes closed. He appeared to be asleep. The nurse said nothing as Margie moved toward him. Probably because he was the patient just admitted to the ward, there was no need to ask whom Margie wanted to see.

Approaching the bed, she asked, "Is he asleep?"

"No."

"Is he able to talk?"

"I'm sure he'd rather not," the nurse said in a low voice. "He's not very comfortable right now."

His hand lay limply over his chest, outside the blanket that was tucked around him. Margie covered his hand with hers; it felt hot and lifeless. "I just wanted to see him for a minute," she whispered to the nurse, but she was looking at Kyle's pale face.

"I understand," the woman said, and backed away from the bedside. She crossed to the other side of the room.

Margie bent over him, not knowing whether or not she should try to talk to him. Softly she whispered his name. His eyes fluttered open reluctantly and he stared up at her, simply stared, and she had no way of knowing whether he even recognized her or not.

"Kyle..." she repeated, and touched his forehead gently. His hand under hers tensed and gripped the sheet, as though he were in pain or greatly disturbed about something.

He winced, and his lips moved. Obviously he wanted to say something. It was an effort, but finally the words came, husky and weak. "I'm sorry...."

Margie looked at him for what seemed a very long time, waiting for something else, but there was nothing else. His eyes closed again.

Finally she asked gently, "Sorry for what?"

"Sorry..." he muttered, and swallowed with difficulty. His hand remained tense, but he didn't open his eyes again or try to speak.

Her shoulders heaved in a helpless sigh. It wasn't possible to push him; he could barely talk. But what, she wondered, was he apologizing for? Something might

have happened at his house tonight before the fire began, but what could that have to do with her?

As she stood looking down at his handsome face in the
soft white light of the room, feeling the heat of his hand
and watching the heave of his chest as he breathed, a
swelling, hideous fear rose in Margie. Did he recognize
her? He had shown no real sign of recognition. Was he
apologizing to her for something, or did he think she was
someone else?

When she whispered his name still again, he moved his
hand and his lips but made no attempt to open his eyes.
Both nurses had said he was in pain; this was all that was
important now.

The nurse approached again. "He's just been given
medication. Hopefully, he'll be able to have a reason-
ably restful night. He should be much better by morning."

Margie nodded numbly. "If I sat with him . . ."

"There's really no need to do that. He'll be all right.
Why don't you get some sleep yourself and come back
tomorrow? He'll be able to talk to you then."

"You're sure he's all right?"

"Yes, quite sure."

When she drew her hand away from over his, her entire body felt suddenly colder. His warmth had penetrated all through her, and now without it the night she
had to go back into was even colder and blacker than
before. For a few minutes longer she stood over him, just
watching him, aching for a response from him, any sign
at all that he knew she was there. None came.

Turning, Margie reluctantly went back to face the
emptiness of the rainy night with the frustration of all its
unanswered questions.

I'm sorry was the only thing he'd said or wanted to say. "You've nothing to apologize to me for, Kyle," she muttered aloud as she drove the long road home from the hospital. "Nothing at all. Who did you think I was?"

It was after midnight by the time she got home. Newton was waiting for her at the door, and the dogs came running in from the living room. How she wished they could talk and tell her what had happened at Kyle's house tonight.

Newton was still unusually restless. Even after Margie was in bed, she could hear him moving about the house. The storm had ceased, so it wasn't the weather that was bothering him. *Tomorrow*, she thought. *Tomorrow Kyle will be able to talk.*

IT HURT to drive past the burned house the next morning. Because it was more than a quarter mile off the road and behind a lane of newly budding trees, Margie could get a look at only a portion of it, enough to see the extensive damage to the blackened roof. One part of her wanted very badly to turn in through his gate and drive up there to have a better look at the damage in the light of day, but a stronger urge wouldn't allow her to do it. Things were depressing enough this morning without that. The house might be completely burned out inside, so much so that it would have to be torn down. Kyle might ask her about the damage, and for this morning at least, it was better that she didn't know what to tell him.

Visiting hours at the hospital didn't begin until ten o'clock. She might be able to see him sooner, but not this much sooner; it was only nine o'clock. Getting some errands out of the way would make the time go faster, she decided, so she pulled into the grocery store, but she never got inside.

Two acquaintances, old school pals, recognized her as soon as she stepped out of the car and greeted her with enthusiasm.

"The whole town's talking about the fire last night!" one of them, Mary Gregg, said. "They say Kyle Sanders was unconscious and isn't expected to live."

Margie swallowed, but the words didn't frighten her after her assurances last night that Kyle was going to recover. Gossip burned out of all proportion around a small town, like a prairie fire in front of a wind.

"I heard he's going to be all right," Margie answered, trying to sound as casual as possible while she adjusted the shoulder strap of her leather handbag.

The other woman, Judy Penney, tugged excitedly at Margie's sleeve. "Have you seen the paper this morning?"

"About the fire? No . . ."

"Not about the fire! About Kyle Sanders! Did you know he *murdered* his wife?"

Margie felt the blood drain from her face. Her knees went so weak she could barely stand. Judy's words hit her like a bomb and the sound of them was exploding in her brain.

All she could manage to say was *"What?"*

"It's true," Mary confirmed. "His wife was killed in a plane crash, and he's suspected of rigging the plane."

Stunned, trying to keep panic from her voice, Margie asked, "Who did this story come from?" She was thinking about Wayne Brockmeier, but surely he *wouldn't* . . . without evidence?

"The name on the story is Bill Stoddard," Judy answered.

Margie remembered the reporter's words last night. *I remember this guy from somewhere*, Stoddard had said.

"It's all in there," Judy continued. "Bill Stoddard used to work in a small town near Omaha and he remembered the story in the Omaha paper five years ago. Last night he phoned Omaha and had them review the details. Just think, Margie—your own neighbor a murderer!"

"If he was a murderer, he'd be in jail," Margie said, fighting to keep her voice below a scream. "Do you have the newspaper?"

"No, I read it at home, but there may be one on the stand by the store. They're selling out fast all over town."

One paper was left in the coin machine. The headline read, "Last Night's Fire Victim Alleged Murder Suspect." Margie's teeth clenched; her armpits began to sweat. No wonder Stoddard wasn't at the hospital. He had remembered where he'd heard Kyle's name and had spent the night writing *this!* Anger seethed within her. This was so damned unfair!

Aware of other people around the market and wanting to get away from her friends, Margie excused herself abruptly, not caring how strange it looked for her to do so. Driving a mile farther to the hospital, she parked in the corner of the lot and read the article through.

It dwelled on the disappearance of Kyle's wife, in far more detail than Kyle had been willing to give her, and it was written with complete bias. No other theory about the woman's disappearance was mentioned besides the weak, ungrounded theory that Kyle might have rigged the plane to crash over impassable mountain terrain. Stoddard was going for sensationalism; the facts were blatantly distorted.

More than anger, Margie felt sick. What right had a reporter to do this? Kyle had come to Rosewood to try to make a new start, and now this had happened. What was worse, the article promised a follow-up story, which meant Stoddard was still digging.

And so was Brockmeier. *I'm next*, Margie thought bitterly. Once these vultures got the scent, there was no stopping them. Kyle wouldn't be able to live and work peacefully in this town now, and before this nightmare was over, she wouldn't be able to, either.

11

FOLDING THE NEWSPAPER carefully and tucking it under the seat, Margie got out of the car and looked at her watch. A quarter to ten. Almost hospital visiting hours. The walk across the parking lot and through the corridor seemed a thousand miles stretching between them. *. . . not expected to live . . .* the rumors were. No, the rumors were wrong! But last night Kyle had looked terrible and been too sick even to talk. The long hours between then and now had been hell for Margie. Endless ticking minutes of restlessness and worry.

The room was bright with sunlight that shone in through the east windows. Kyle was propped on two pillows, lying with one arm over his eyes. The short-sleeved hospital gown looked very unnatural on him, and there were strange bruises on his arms. Margie was overcome with a sense of unreality, as if this whole thing—last night and this morning and the fire and the newspaper and the hospital—were a dream and not happening at all.

When she touched his arm, he jerked in alarm.

"Oh! I didn't mean to startle you, Kyle."

His eyes opened. "Margie. Thank God. I thought you were another nurse."

"I've been worried sick. Are you all right?"

"Hell, I don't know."

"They tell me you're going to live."

"They tell me that, too, but I feel like hell."

"Why wouldn't you feel like hell? You've been through a lot." She set down her handbag on the overbed table. "What are these bruises on your arms?"

"I've got bruises all over my body. Can't even move without moaning."

"Bruises from what?"

He chose to ignore the question. "And my throat hurts."

"The paramedics put a tube down your throat to help you breathe. You were unconscious.... Kyle, what *are* all the bruises from?"

Rubbing the stubble of beard over his chin, he merely looked at her. She sat down on the edge of the high bed and waited. The two other patients in the ward were awake, sitting up in their beds and within easy earshot of what she and Kyle were saying. They were listening to every word. Perhaps that was why he hesitated to answer. She leaned forward and whispered, "There's no privacy here."

"Tell me about it. I had a public bath in bed this morning." He squirmed with discomfort. "I hate hospitals. I have to get out of here."

"The bruises?" she reminded him in a sympathetic voice, touching his upper arm gently with her fingertips over a dark blue bruise. "Did you fall ...?"

Brushing the hair from his eyes in frustration, he said, "Newton."

"Newton? What do you mean, Newton?"

"The bruises are from Newton."

"Kyle! He wouldn't hurt you! He—"

"He didn't do it to hurt me, Margie: he saved my life."

Too stunned to answer, she merely sat in silence and looked at him.

"He pushed me out of the house with sheer force. I couldn't even walk. Newton kept jabbing me and shoving me until I thought I couldn't stand it. I'd fallen asleep by the fire, and he must have broken the door down, because he'd been outside on the porch. I'd shut him out there."

"Newton saved your life?"

"Yeah. I was saved by a pig." Kyle sighed shakily, and swallowed carefully with a wince, a reminder to Margie that he'd said his throat was very sore.

She took his hand. He hadn't smiled at the admission he was saved by a pig. He hadn't smiled at all since she'd walked into the room.

He raised her hand to his lips and kissed her fingers with affection, then lay back against the pillows and closed his eyes. "How much is left of my house? Have you seen it?"

"Not this morning."

"I asked a nurse to call the fire department to find out the extent of the damage. It doesn't sound good." His eyes were still closed. He muttered, "Damn..."

"I thought about going over there on my way to town, but somehow I just couldn't."

"When did you get back from your trip?"

"Last night, just before the ambulance arrived to bring you to the hospital. I saw the smoke from the road."

He scowled. "You were there last night?"

"Yes, and here at the hospital, too. You lost consciousness from smoke inhalation and no one knew how serious it was and I was scared to death. I never would have imagined you'd be so much better this morning."

"Better? I feel like I've been dragged and battered by a giant carnivore and spent the night breathing fire."

She smiled softly. "I'll admit you look a little sick. What happened to start the fire, do you know?"

He shrugged. "A spark on the rug, maybe. Or a log falling out. I don't know. I just remember Newton jabbing me under the arms and he was hurting me like hell. He refused to let me lie there. I became aware of smoke and then flames, but I could barely move."

"Smoke inhalation."

"Yeah. That and the fact that I was drunk as an owl."

Her eyes opened wide in surprise. "You were drunk?"

"We both were."

"Both who?"

"Newton and I were drunk."

"Oh, no."

He looked directly into her eyes. "It's not fun telling you this, Margie, but that's what happened. Newton was sozzled, and I was dead tired...."

"You might have died last night!"

"That's what the hospital staff has been telling me. Another few minutes was probably all I would have lasted. Ol' Newton's got a constitution I haven't. He smelled smoke and came after me. I recall his pushing me and King barking, and me trying to get to the door and thinking I couldn't."

She studied his bruised arm for some seconds longer, then looked up at him. "Why did you and Newton start drinking?"

"We didn't...I mean, not together. I left the back-porch door open so he could get in out of the rain, not remembering that I had a case of beer stored out there. When I got home from work, he'd finished off the case and was staggering around laughing and trying to lick up whatever he'd spilled. Punctured those beer cans like they were made of paper. I was so disgusted, I decided if you can't beat 'em, join 'em, and after a rotten day at work, I was ready for a drink anyhow. A couple drinks on an empty stomach knocked me out. You know the rest. I sat by the fire and fell asleep and my house burned down."

She sighed. "That's great."

"My middle name is trouble. Kyle T. Sanders." Lying back limply on the pillow, he sighed shakily.

She asked, "Does it hurt to talk?"

"No, just to swallow."

"How are you otherwise, other than the bruises, I mean? Have they said how long you have to stay in the hospital?"

"Just today. They took X rays of my chest last night, and I guess there's no reason to think I'll die. They'd probably let me out today if—" He hesitated and scowled.

"If what?"

"If I had a home to go back to."

"I don't know how badly damaged your house is, but you can stay with me."

"Gossip will run rampant."

"At this point, who cares what—" Margie began, and stopped because she was interrupted by the doctor.

The tall, gray-haired physician ambled leisurely to the bedside accompanied by a nurse and stood with his hands in his pockets, smiling. "How are you feeling this morning, Kyle? I hear you didn't sleep too well."

"How could I sleep when you people kept waking me to see if I was alive?"

The doctor laughed as if there was some humor in Kyle's complaint and glanced at Margie. "I'd like a few minutes to examine my patient, if you wouldn't mind waiting outside."

"No, of course not." Her voice was weak and shaking.

Kyle, noticing the strange look on her face, asked, "Is something wrong, Margie?"

She tried unsuccessfully to smile. "I'll . . . just wait outside for the doctor to finish, and then I'll . . . be . . . back. . . ."

She turned toward the door, quietly recoiling from dread. The doctor had a Rosewood newspaper tucked under his arm! Why would he bring the newspaper into this room unless he intended to show it to Kyle?

How was he going to react to those headlines? Margie paced the corridor nervously, repeatedly returning to the coffee machine and then leaving the strong black coffee to cool in the cup. Every couple of minutes she glanced at her watch. Fifteen minutes passed, then twenty, before the doctor and the nurse opened the door of the ward.

The doctor shot her an odd glance she couldn't interpret before he continued down the hall with his assistant, talking in tones too low for her to hear. Margie stood still, watching them.

She tried to calm herself. It would have been only a matter of time anyway—hours at the longest—before someone showed Kyle the paper. The doctor knew that, of course. Obviously, he wanted to question Kyle about it. As well as Margie knew the man she loved, she couldn't guess for certain how he'd reacted to seeing that article. She only knew she dreaded finding out.

It was quiet in the room except for the voices of the two other patients, who were talking softly. Kyle lay with his eyes closed and didn't hear her come in. Margie stood by the bed, just stood there, trying to decide what to say.

There didn't seem to be anything to say. She touched his hand. His eyes opened slowly, and what she saw in them, Margie didn't like. Her first impulse was to draw back.

After a strange silence, he said, "You didn't tell me about the newspaper."

"I was going to. There were more important things on my mind."

"More important than everybody in Rosewood believing I'm a murderer?"

"Yes. How you are is more important. When I saw you last night you seemed more dead than alive."

The shine of anger was in his light eyes. That frightening anger again. "Who is this reporter who has taken it upon himself to crucify me?"

"His name, as you saw on the byline, is Bill Stoddard. I know nothing about him except he's only been in town a year or so, and he was there at the fire last night taking pictures. He was taking pictures of you—including the one on the second page, the one of them lifting you into the ambulance."

"That's a great picture. I appreciate it a lot."

"He said he thought he knew you from someplace, recognized your name." Margie hugged her arms at the memory and shuddered. "I had a bad feeling about him last night."

"This Stoddard doesn't like to make any distinction between fact and fiction," Kyle muttered through clenched teeth. "He picked the wrong guy to go after."

A rumble of fear went through her. "What are you going to do, Kyle? The story is already out. What can you do about it now?"

"I don't know. I'll think of something, you can bet on it." He shrugged in frustration, then winced because it hurt to move. "I swear that pig broke half my ribs."

"Kyle . . ."

"I know. I know, Margie. Fighting with Stoddard isn't going to help anything. I'm just . . . I'm so sick of it, of all of it. I told the doctor I'm going home. He asked where that was, now that the fire department says I can't move back into the house until they do some more inspecting. I told him not to worry about it, that I was leaving the hospital."

"What did he say to that?"

Kyle hesitated. "Do I have to tell the truth?"

"Yes."

"He said I should stay here because I . . . need to rest."

There was no way to stop herself from reaching to him. Her heart was aching for him. Touching his cheek gently, she said, "Of course you need rest. You can rest at my house."

"Margie, I can't . . . ."

"You can, and you will. Kyle, if *my* house had burned, could I stay with you?"

"Naturally, but—"

"Well, I don't want you with anyone but me. I'm going to take care of you."

"I don't think you ought to associate with me. It would be bad enough my staying there without people thinking I'm a murderer."

"I don't care what people say."

"That's not true, Margie. You care very much what people say."

"Maybe I need to put things in perspective, then. I care more about you than I care about them. You and I are more important . . . than they are."

He squeezed her hand with affection and gazed at her eyes. "The fire was a needless accident."

"You fell asleep. You can sleep very soundly, Kyle. I've tried uselessly to shake you awake sometimes."

"We both know—"

Gently her fingertips covered his lips. "We both know it was an accident, and there's no point in discussing it further. When are you leaving the hospital?"

Kyle rubbed his hand over his stubble of beard. "Margie, listen to me. I'm still thinking of you, your reputation and the fact that I'm . . . a married man."

The words jolted her; she almost reeled. He still thought of himself as married. She stared at him. "*Are* you a married man?"

"To the best of my knowledge I am."

"And that matters to you. . . ."

"Only out of concern for you. With this newspaper story out, everybody is going to know I'm married."

"That wasn't exactly the gist of the story, Kyle. The story was about your wife being dead, remember? The 'missing' part was glossed over pretty well. And anyway, I told you, I'm not going to sit around worrying about wagging tongues. Not anymore."

Kyle remained hesitant. "Since when?"

"Since you."

His eyes filled with a mixture of sadness and admiration.

Margie said, "You need me, Kyle, so please don't give me a hard time. Right now you need me and I'm here, and there isn't anything else to discuss. Except when you're leaving the hospital. You didn't answer about when you're leaving."

Kyle smiled surrender. She was right, he thought; he did need her, in more ways than she knew. "As soon as they get me some release papers and somebody tells me what they've done with my clothes."

"All right. I have to pick up a few things at the store and then I'll come back for you. It shouldn't take me much more than a half hour."

He closed his eyes. "You're sure you want to do this?"

"Do I look like the kind of person who isn't sure?"

"If I just . . . if I just felt better . . ."

"Give yourself time. Is it so terrible to . . . need someone, if only for a little while?"

He opened his eyes and gazed at her with an expression that was hard for her to read. "It's different. I'm not used to it."

"I know. Do you think you could get used to it?"

"No."

"Okay. You don't have to try. Take one day at a time. Just get rested. You need time to get well." She turned to leave. "And right now try to find your clothes."

WHEN SHE PULLED UP in front of the hospital forty-five minutes later, Kyle was sitting alone at the top of the stairs waiting for her. Wearing faded jeans and a sooty tan shirt, he was barefoot and unshaven, and in his hand he was holding a single red rose.

He didn't give her time to get out of the car. As soon as she stopped, he was off the step and walking toward her, but his walk wasn't his normal one. Each step was slow and deliberate, as if he hurt all over.

Would this have happened, Margie wondered, if Newton wasn't so prone to mischief? If he hadn't found the beer stored on the back porch? Might Kyle have come home from work and had a few drinks and fallen asleep in front of the fire anyway? Did Newton cause this whole thing, or was Kyle alive today only because Newton happened to be there?

Kyle handed her the rose as he got into the car. Its subtle fragrance blended with the freshness of a spring morning after a night of rain.

The gesture warmed her, thrilled her. "Where did you ever find a rose?"

"In the gift shop. They were willing to put it on my hospital bill. It's a small gift for a big favor."

"What favor?"

He smiled about it. Finally. "Taking in a bum with no ID, filthy clothes and no shoes."

Glancing at him, Margie started the engine. "I guess we should stop at your house and get you something to wear."

"Maybe there's nothing left that isn't charred."

"Oh, Kyle, do you think it's that bad?"

"The fireman's voice was fairly dripping with sympathy. Twice he mentioned the fact that the ranch is so far from the fire station. Almost twenty minutes. And no one has determined how long the fire had been going before neighbors noticed and phoned it in. There was a lot of damage done before the fire trucks got there, so I'm not too optimistic." He heaved a sigh. "I don't think I'm up to going home just yet. I'm not ready to face it. When I stand up, everything gets whirly and dark and I feel like I'm going to throw up. I hope I don't throw up in your car."

"If you do, don't worry about it."

The bright sunlight emphasized how pale he looked, even worse now, Margie thought, than before he read the story about himself in the morning paper. Margie knew he was holding back his anger over the story for her sake.

By the time they were through town and on the country road, he had lapsed into silence. A glance in his direction confirmed that he had fallen asleep with his head resting against the window and supported by his left arm.

He still slept as they passed by his house, and Margie was glad of that. It was difficult to look down the lane where that dark green roof had always been and see only charred rafters. The tops of two tall trees that stood in the yard nearest the house were burned. And there was an awful deathlike silence over everything.

Margie glanced at Kyle in sleep, at his hand curled under his head, noted his breathing, which was labored for someone asleep, his hair in his eyes, the heavy stubble of beard. She thought how handsome he was. And how strong. And how filled with pain that lingered on year after year, pain that he'd never learned to deal with. And now this . . . now perhaps he'd lost his home on top of everything else.

When she stopped in her driveway, he sat up groggily and looked about, dazed for a second or two, to find his bearings.

Margie said, "You need to just get into bed and sleep."

"I guess so."

"Are you hungry?"

"No."

"I could fix a little something. . . ."

"Swallowing isn't too easy." He opened the car door.

Stiffly and slowly, he entered the house to the enthusiastic greetings of his dog. Pig Newton stood back snorting softly with an I-won't-tell-her-we-were-drunk-if-you-don't look on his face.

Kyle gave him a pat on the head. "It's not much of a thank-you for saving my life. Not every guy is lucky enough to have such a courageous buddy."

The dog nipped at him affectionately. "You, too, King. You guys were heroes and I'm not gonna dwell on what I was last night—not in front of my lady."

Margie held the door open and shooed all three animals outside. The sun was shining now over a fine spring morning. "I'm going to turn down the bed for you."

"Better make it the guest bed in case you have callers, after the whole valley has read the newspaper story about me. There are excited tongues flapping this morning."

"Yes, I suppose there are."

She went into her guest room and turned down the bed. Moments later Kyle walked in naked and slid between the sheets. Margie sat on the bed and examined his bare chest. "Good heavens, you're black and blue!"

"I guess it's a small price to pay for being alive." Gently, her hand pushed the hair away from his eyes and lingered for several seconds longer on his forehead. He felt hot, as if he had a fever; no doubt it was a fever. "I'll look in on you later to see if you need anything."

He caught her hand in his and kissed her fingertips. "You're babying me."

"Yes, I am. Any objections?"

"I'm not . . . used to it."

"I know. Just for now let me take care of you."

SHADOWS OF DUSK descended over the room, and still he slept. He had turned onto his stomach, his arms above his head. She rested her hand on his bare back and gently began to rub his shoulders.

He stirred and sighed a little moan of pleasure.

"Feeling any better?" she asked softly.

"Dunno yet, but that feels damn good."

"Kyle . . . I have to talk to you. Wayne Brockmeier phoned from Florida an hour ago. He tried to call your house and your phone was disconnected. And no one answered at your office. So he called here and asked me if you'd left for Florida yet. *Yet*—as if it were a fact of life that you'd be going down there."

Kyle shifted, frowning. "To Florida?"

She nodded, noting the sudden darkening of his eyes. "What is in Florida?"

He became pensive and farther from her. Even though he hadn't moved an inch, Margie felt as if he were suddenly farther away.

He answered, "I don't know what's in Florida. Brockmeier went there looking for—" He looked down at the bed.

"For your wife?"

"Yeah."

Her eyes grew wide and her heart began to beat faster. "Do you think there's a chance he's found her?"

"It's hard to say. He could have found . . . a tombstone for all I know. Or maybe he hasn't found anything and just wants to get my reaction—or your reaction. He isn't above theatrics."

She chewed on her thumbnail nervously. "Is there any way for you to find out?"

"Probably. My attorney in Omaha is in touch with the private detective we hired. My guy got to Florida before Brockmeier did. Following some rumor." He combed back his hair hurriedly with his fingers. "What time is it?"

"Nearly seven."

"I'll have to call Horace at home. He had no way of getting me today, either, if there *was* anything to tell me."

He tossed aside the sheet and drew his husky legs to the side of the bed opposite where she was sitting. "I'd better phone Omaha, though, in case Brockmeier isn't bluffing and there really is something going on."

"Your clothes are there on the chair. I managed to get the soot out of your shirt." Her voice was numb as stark reality took hold. In the course of only a few hours there'd been the fire, fear for Kyle's life, the terrible newspaper headlines and now this, now Brockmeier... now Claire.

He used the phone in the den. Margie tried to busy herself, but her curiosity was so great she couldn't help but eavesdrop on his side of the conversation with his attorney.

"Horace, I got word that Wayne Brockmeier is trying to get hold of me from somewhere in Florida. Do you know anything about it? Damn, I was afraid you might have. There's been some trouble out here. My phone lines are down.... No, I'll explain later.... What about John Dillon?"

Margie paced about and tried to stay calm, but each moment the effort tripled. Kyle listened, his face blank. The man on the other end talked at length.

Kyle said suddenly, "Even before you told *me*?"

There was another very long pause while he listened. His face revealed no emotion at all, although his eyes were squinting strangely, an expression Margie had never seen.

"You're damned right I am," Kyle said into the phone. He frowned then. "I don't know how soon. I'm not feeling too good, Horace; I spent last night in the hospital sick as a dog.... No, no, I'll explain later.... Where's Dillon now? How do I contact him?"

His voice had gone flat. And his face had paled. Watching him, Margie felt something go all hollow inside her. This was it, then. This was the answer Kyle had waited five years for—it had to be. And the timing was terrible; he was too sick for this today.

It was impossible for her to tell from the one-sided conversation what Kyle had just learned about his wife. Margie sat in dread, feeling as if every ounce of strength had just been drained from her body. His face remained so blank, so strangely blank. Frightened, she sat on the den couch, drew up her knees and hugged them tightly.

Kyle scribbled something on the notepad by the phone. His hand trembled as he wrote, and perspiration dampened the paper and streaked the ink.

"Okay, Horace, I hear you. Yes, damn it, I hear you! What d'you mean, I sound feverish? Hell, I *am* feverish! You're not helping." His voice rose with impatience. "There's no need for that...."

After another anxious pause of listening, he said finally, "Okay. I'll let you know, or Dillon will. One of us will."

When he hung up, Kyle sat staring into space, stunned, trying to absorb what he had heard. Realizing this, Margie waited in silence. Perspiration dampened her armpits.

He gazed up at her at last and met her eyes. His voice was a monotone when he spoke. "They've found Claire."

Margie felt drowned in the ensuing silence, but at last she managed to ask, "She's alive?"

He nodded, rubbing the stubble of beard on his chin, glancing away and then back to her again. "She's living in Miami under an assumed name and she still doesn't know she's been discovered. It was my detective, John Dillon, who found her and he contacted Brockmeier."

"He contacted them before he contacted you?"

"Yeah. Horace has been talking with the insurance company, too. We have to do everything we can to squelch any ideas they may have about my knowing anything about her." He rose and began to pace, walking very stiffly, as if every step was an effort. "Keep it all out in the open, Horace says. If he repeats that one more time..."

Because his body was sore all over, Kyle sat down again. "Honey, I have to go to Florida."

"I know."

"I have to see her."

"Kyle, is there going to be trouble in Florida?"

He looked over at her. "Trouble?"

"I have this awful feeling there's going to be trouble."

He clenched his jaw tightly. "I'm going to find out why Claire did this to me. You don't do things like this to another person...and especially not to someone who loves you."

Margie closed her eyes against the swift, icy impact of his words. He loved his wife; he'd just said so. The jolt caused her head to swim. Kyle had been—still was—deeply hurt by his wife's mysterious disappearance.

"When do you have to leave?"

"As soon as I can."

"Tomorrow?"

"Or tonight. I'd better phone and see what kind of connections I can get from Omaha. How often does the Rosewood puddle jumper fly to Omaha?"

"The evening flight will have already left. I think the next one leaves Rosewood around six in the morning."

"Do you have a phone book?"

"I'll get your reservations for you," she offered, rising on unsteady legs. *Don't go!* she wanted to plead, but of course she wouldn't say it. And even if she said it, it wouldn't do any good; he had to go. The woman they'd found in Florida was his wife. And anything could happen when they saw each other again.

PREOCCUPIED WITH PRIVATE THOUGHTS that couldn't be shared and still in pain, Kyle was not quite himself the rest of the evening. There was the trauma, too, of having to return to his house and survey the damage from the fire.

The living room was burned out. The bedrooms in the south wing were mostly intact, but smoke and water had done serious damage.

He swore softly as he shone his flashlight into his charred closet. "Everything smells of smoke. I can't wear these clothes to anything but a fire."

"It's too late to shop. I can try to wash something."

He gathered up two pairs of jeans and some socks and underwear from a drawer. "I'll try, if you'll let me use your machine. My shoes are just going to have to stink."

From a closet shelf, he lifted down a suitcase and threw the clothes inside, with a wallet and checkbook and watch that were on the dresser top. The wallet and checkbook were damp and stiff. "This is depressing, Margie. Let's go."

Over their late dinner, he was quieter than usual. His mind was on other things, and he was not inclined to talk about tomorrow or what he might find once he reached Miami.

Margie asked, "Does finding Claire mean the insurance company will be off your back now?"

"I don't know. Claire could lie and implicate me if she wanted to. God knows what she'll do."

"Might she run away again?"

"We've got to prevent that from happening."

"Kyle," she began carefully, "how do you feel...when you think of her?"

"Feel?"

"What emotion comes to mind first?"

He shrugged slightly. "Anger. Long bottled-up anger."

A shiver of fear came over her. This wasn't going to be easy for him.

"You're not eating much," she observed.

"I'm not feeling that great. I think I'd better get to bed before I fall on my face. Come to bed with me, Margie? If only to hold each other? I think we need to hold each other tonight."

Moisture formed in her eyes. Until he said it, she hadn't realized—hadn't dared even think about—how much she wanted him to hold her, just hold her, and make the night belong only to them.

Tomorrow he would be with his wife again.

12

WAITING FOR the boarding call, Kyle was very quiet. He held her hand in the eerie silence of the tiny airport. The eastern sky was orange and the day was calm without a breath of wind. Birds sang songs of spring outside, in a greening world. And Margie thought, *this is the day he's leaving me. It will never be the same again.*

"Margie," he said as if he were reading the thoughts behind the sadness on her face, "I'll come back to you. I love you."

His goodbye kiss was gentle. He held her tightly against his body and their hearts beat together, and in those moments, the fear lessened for her.

But when he pulled away, it returned at once and remained as she watched him walk out onto the tarmac and board the plane.

He turned once, and there was a strange sadness in his smile; that smile was almost forced. Margie couldn't help but wonder if Kyle, too, felt that things were never going to be the same once he stepped on that plane.

WORK WAS THE BEST ANSWER to the frustration of waiting for time to pass. It was a good day to spend at her office catching up on paperwork. There were errands to run in town, too, although it was too early to do them; businesses wouldn't open for another two or three hours. Kyle had asked her to stop by his office to pick up and mail a set of blueprints and some letters, which she could do on the way to the auction barn.

Main Street was deserted at this time of morning except for a street-sweeping machine that swished by, disturbing the calm of sunrise. A paperboy wearing red earmuffs against the morning chill was riding his bicycle along the sidewalk, tossing morning papers from his basket to the entrances of closed stores. Margie pulled into a parking space in front of the bank and with Kyle's key let herself into the door that led directly from the street to the second-story stairway.

To her surprise, the door of his office was unlocked. Perhaps the cleaning woman had been in, or else Kyle had simply neglected to lock it, knowing the building was well secured at the outside door.

A light was on inside. Margie remembered his telling her how wrung out he'd been when he left his office the night before last. He'd probably left in a hurry.

It was eerie in the old bank building at this early hour. The steam radiators creaked and moaned. Stale odors of dust and cigar and cigarette smoke permeated the very walls. Kyle's desk was piled high with paperwork, but the outgoing letters were easy enough to locate because they were leaning upright between a stapler and a pencil holder. She found the blueprints in the drawer where Kyle said they would be and was double-checking to make sure they were the right ones when the ringing of the telephone startled her. Why would anyone be calling here at this hour?

Margie picked up the phone after the third ring. "Kyle Sanders's office."

"That you, Miss Donovan?"

Her pulse quickened. It was Brockmeier's voice.

"Yes."

"Let me speak to Kyle."

"He isn't here."

Clearly, he didn't believe her. "Come on now. This is important."

"Kyle isn't here. I just came in to pick up some blueprints this morning."

"Where is he?"

"I'm not going to tell you anything, Mr. Brockmeier."

"You're mad at me."

Her eyes rolled toward the ceiling. "I don't appreciate being implicated in suspicions of murder. Would you?"

"It's my job not to overlook any lead. If you're so innocent, why won't you cooperate?"

"Because you're dead wrong."

"About you and Kyle knowing each other before Rosewood? Meeting in Europe? No, I don't think so. Our people in Europe have found some hospital records in Paris. You gave birth to a daughter in Paris during a week when Sanders was not in Amsterdam with his wife. We know there was a man with you. We just have to prove it was Kyle. There's strong motivation for conspiracy, Miss Donovan, if you and Sanders have a child. He wouldn't have wanted his wife to learn about that, would he? I haven't found out yet where your child is, but there was a call to my home office from France this morning, so chances are they've learned something else."

"You're completely wrong! You're—" Margie paused because the words were fumbling on her tongue. "I happen to know, Mr. Brockmeier, that Claire Sanders is alive. So why the devil are you still looking for motivation for her murder?"

"We're looking for conspiracy. Blackmail. Fraud. We don't believe Claire Sanders was capable of pulling off this disappearing act alone, and it's her husband who stood to profit from it."

"None of that has anything to do with me."

"I'm not at all convinced of that. Especially if you two were involved enough to have a child together, and obviously you are still very involved...."

"We don't have a child!"

"Whose child was it, then, that you gave birth to in Paris, if not his?"

Margie paled. Her hands were shaking. "How dare you violate my privacy this way! I think you've overstepped your legal bounds and I intend to find out if you have."

"You're not going to do anything to call attention to it, though, are you? I doubt you'd want to draw public attention to something you've kept concealed for so long." He waited for a response that didn't come and then said, "I think I've found the answer to my question. Since you know about Claire Sanders being found, then I have to assume Kyle is already on his way down here."

"Assume anything you like."

"Yes, well. You and I probably won't have the pleasure of talking again, unless it's in a court of law. Goodbye, Miss Donovan."

Trembling, Margie hung up the phone. She sat in Kyle's chair, elbows on his desk, and buried her face in her hands. Tears were welling in her eyes.

A shuffling sound came from the other side of the alcove. She looked up, startled, then horrified, to see Bill Stoddard standing in the archway smiling.

Margie wiped at her eyes self-consciously. "Where did you come from? What are you doing here?"

"Doing here? Looking around for anything that might be of interest in my follow-up story. The door was unlocked so I let myself in. Can't be called breaking and entering if the door was unlocked, can it? I've been in the other room, listening on the phone extension."

Margie's heart sank. She stared at him, open-mouthed.

Stoddard grinned. "I got a hell of a bigger story than I bargained for."

"If you dare print one word of that phone conversation..."

"You'll do what? It sounds to me like the information is verifiable."

"That phone conversation was a lie!"

He laughed. "Come on. Everybody suspects there's something going on between you and Kyle Sanders. Now there's proof. He was married and you got pregnant by him and went to Europe so nobody in your hometown would know. This is a *scoop!* Sanders's wife is alive after all, huh? She's in your way again, is she? Do you want to tell me where she is? Where *he* is? I might tread lighter over your reputation in my story if you help me out with that information."

"Get out of here!"

"Hey, I mean what I just said. You can trust me. Just tell me where she is."

"I'm warning you," Margie said, almost choking. "If you print one word of any of this, you'll wish you hadn't."

"I don't scare. And I don't throw away sensational headlines." He looked at his watch. "And I haven't got time to stand here, if you won't listen to reason. I've got a story to write for tomorrow's paper!"

He slithered out like a serpent, not bothering to close the door behind him. Margie sat in shock. Everything had come to a head like a festering boil. Below the windows, in the street, were sounds of a town waking. A delivery truck, a dog barking, voices of men off-loading boxes down a ramp. It sounded to Margie as if the noises were far away, in another world where she didn't belong anymore. The walls of Kyle's office seemed to close in on her. It would do no good to try to reason with the publisher; this was the news story of the decade. And now that Stoddard knew about her past, however distorted, the town would know within hours. She could deny the story about her and Kyle. But where would it get her? There was too much proof of the overlying facts of her past. She'd only get in deeper by trying to claw her way out. How she was going to deal with this, she didn't know. Kyle would be with his wife tomorrow, when Stoddard's story broke. With aching bitterness, Margie remembered what it was like to feel utterly alone.

THANK GOD for her companions, Margie thought during the long evening while she felt she was waiting for her own execution by the press. Pig Newton and Angel were there for her, sticking by her with loyal devotion. King, too, had made himself at home in her house, and in the quietest moments he was the most affectionate of all.

With the passing of each hour, Margie discovered more about herself. She was far less apprehensive about tomorrow's newspaper story than she was about what was happening in Miami. Kyle's reunion with his wife was what frightened her. The rest she could deal with if she had to. And obviously she had to. It was too soon to try to predict what all of it meant to her future. The future from this vantage point was very murky and dark. Far into the night Margie's mind raced with a thousand scenarios, a thousand possibilities that blackened her dreams with fear.

DRESSED IN NEWLY PURCHASED slacks and a lightweight sport jacket, Kyle entered the dimly lit club in the heart of Miami's nightlife district and tipped the waiter ten dollars to give him a table near the stage.

"Tell Amber Carlson the admirer who sent the roses is in the audience and would like to buy her a drink."

The waiter, who spoke with a Spanish accent, looked at him without any expression whatsoever, nodded and led him to a small table in the front.

The club was less than half-full, but it was early still. Maybe, Kyle thought, the crowd came later or maybe there never was a crowd in here. The place was anything but impressive—small and musty with the smell of stale smoke. A dive, nothing but a cheap dive. The last place on earth he expected to find Claire.

Yet something about it rang strangely true. She'd always talked about wanting a career as a singer, fantasized about it, sung all the time when she was alone. She had sometimes dreamed grand dreams of becoming a famous singer. But this—this club featured strippers on the program. Surely Claire hadn't sunk deep enough into the mire to be stripping, too. . . .

Kyle was forced to sit, fidgeting, through a strip act of two blond twins with rhinestone G-strings. The next performance, a female impersonator, was even worse. By the time it was over, Kyle, anticipating seeing his wife on that narrow, paint-chipped stage, was sweating profusely and his hands felt cold.

When she did appear, as Amber Carlson, he sat back, stunned. Wearing a long white gown, cut straight and plain below small rhinestone straps, with her dark hair dyed a shining amber, Claire walked out on the stage in a spotlight like a queen entering a ballroom. Tall and slim, her once-straight hair curling softly about her face, she waltzed to the piano, smiled at the piano player, a young man in a faded tuxedo, turned toward the audience and waited for the introduction to her song.

Kyle forgot to breathe. It was Claire, but it wasn't— this blond woman who began to sing in a strong, melodious voice. He remembered the voice the moment she began to sing; he'd listened to it often enough in the evenings when she was preparing their dinner or in the mornings when she was in the shower. Claire's voice, and yet it wasn't. It sounded different now, stronger, prettier.

And she was beautiful. More beautiful than he remembered. He couldn't glance away for even a second as she delivered a song that sounded familiar to him but that he couldn't identify. She brought a touch of class to this sleazy club. Kyle gradually began to realize there was little talking in the audience while she was singing.

But *why*? Why would she work in a place like this? The experience of sitting here watching her had every characteristic of a nightmare. There had been scores of nightmares during the five years since he saw her last, but this one he wasn't going to be able to wake up from.

Because of the spotlight, he was certain she was unable to see him. Amber Carlson didn't look directly at her audience, anyway, but aloofly past them, as though she were singing to people in a balcony, but there was no balcony. There was only the uncrowded, smoke-filled room with glass beads hanging in the doorways. The shifting light on the stage reflected on the colored beads from time to time and they sparkled when they moved.

He wondered if she would accept his invitation. From the attitude of the waiter, he assumed she would. If she didn't, he'd have to find her backstage, but it would be far better in a public place, where her demure image had to be maintained.

Her first performance of the evening was short. He counted only four songs. Afterward, taking a restrained bow, she left the stage by a small set of stairs on the right. The waiter pointed out his table.

Kyle stood.

In the dim light he could see the signs of recognition come into her face, something not unlike horror at first. Then, conscious that her audience was watching her, Amber Carlson fought for composure, forced a small smile and made her way slowly toward the tall, handsome man who was waiting for her at a table near the stage.

He smiled and held her chair for her. Stiffly, she sat down across from him and merely stared.

"Hello, Claire."

"Hello, Kyle."

He motioned for the waiter to bring her preferred drink, which the waiter knew and Kyle didn't. "I'm impressed. Shocked as hell, but impressed."

"You sent the roses?"

"I remembered you like red roses and this is, after all, a reunion."

Her hands were clutched tightly together over the table. "How did you find me?"

"Does it matter?"

"Yes." She looked around nervously. "Are you alone? Does anyone know you're here?"

"Who do you mean by anyone?"

"I mean, does anyone else know that you found me?"

"What difference does it make?"

"All the difference. Damn it, Kyle! It's been years. I didn't think you'd still be trying to find me. I thought you'd think...I was dead."

"I've never thought you were dead."

"Why not? The plane—"

She stopped as the waiter brought her Scotch, with water on the side. She poured one into the other absently and took a large swallow.

Kyle finished her last sentence for her. "The plane was never found, of course."

Sitting back, taking a swallow from his glass, he felt the tenseness in his body. Claire was a shade or two paler than she had been when she was onstage. Her hands trembled as she picked up her glass.

Trying to keep his voice even and calm, he cocked his head and studied her. Something was wrong. She seemed frightened of him. Claire had never been frightened of him.

Kyle hadn't known his feelings when he came into the club. Curiosity had overpowered everything else, even the seething anger. Self-protection was in play, too. He didn't know his feelings yet, but whatever they were, Kyle didn't want to give them away. He himself had too much to sort out. He needed information and he needed time.

"You look very different, Claire. You're as lovely as ever, but I prefer you as a brunette. What a surprise to find you on a stage belting out songs."

His wife blinked at him from across the table. Her nervousness was obvious, but she, too, was making an effort to stay calm, if only for the sake of the people who sat around them—her audience.

"I'd like to say you look wonderful, Kyle, but in all honesty, you look...older."

"I'm a hell of a lot older. And tired." He leaned onto the table, then closer to her, and his eyes narrowed. "Who are you hiding from, Claire, if not from me?"

"What?"

"Your concern about whether or not anyone else knows your whereabouts, other than me. Who else are you worried about? The insurance company?"

The woman sipped her Scotch. "You're confusing me. I'm so shocked to see you, and you act so casual, as if it had been only yesterday. Why are you acting so strange?"

He scowled. "Claire, for the love of God, what do you want me to do? Will you stop glancing around the room like you're afraid someone will see us? I *am* your husband, you know. Why the hell do you keep looking behind my shoulders?"

"They may have followed you."

"Who?"

She hesitated. "Insurance people or police. I can't sit here, Kyle. I have to sing again soon. I have to go."

As she started to rise, Kyle caught her hand in a firm grip. "You're not going anywhere until I get some answers."

"Please. Not here. Let go of me."

"Yes, right here. Right now. From the beginning, Claire. I want to know why you left me and wanted me and the world to think you were dead."

His demands seemed to frighten her. "No, I . . . can't."

"You can and you will, before you leave this table."

She stared at him, then blinked. "Are you alone?"

"Do you see anyone with me?"

"Why did you keep looking for me?"

"Why did you leave?"

Claire's shoulders sagged in defeat, a gesture that said better than words that now she had been found, the pretense was no good anymore.

He said, "You may as well tell me. I'll find out anyway, one way or another."

"I . . . I want to tell you. Because if you know, then we can . . . we can make it work. We can work together. Can't we?"

He eyed her suspiciously, then his expression abruptly changed and he answered, "Sure."

"We can?"

"Sure."

Relaxing at this reassurance, Claire simply gazed at her husband for a time, chin resting on the palm of her hand, as if her thoughts were somewhere else, in another place, another time. She began, "There was a man. . . ."

"I figured as much."

"He said he wanted to manage my singing career. You didn't know about my singing career, Kyle, but I always wanted that. Well, I talked to you sometimes about wanting to be a singer. . . ."

"Who was he?"

"A man I met through a friend at work. . . ." She took a few sips of her drink while he waited. "We sort of . . . fell in love. He found out one day about our life insurance. . . ."

"I see. And started scheming ways to collect it? You picked a damned strange way—"

"At first he wanted to find a way to . . . I can barely say it, Kyle. He wanted to kill you and make it look like an accident. But of course I wouldn't listen to such talk. I loved you. You were always so kind to me, Kyle, and you would never have hurt *me*. I couldn't let Damon hurt you!"

"Go on."

"Well, I told him that, and so he—that is, we—came up with this better idea to get the money. *I* would be the one presumed dead, you see, and hide until you collected the money, which Damon said would take seven years. Seven years isn't that long to wait for two million dollars."

He gazed now in disbelief. "And after I collected the money, how did Damon plan to get it from me?"

"He was only going to take half. That was *my* absolute stipulation. You would get half and we would get half. That way, you'd have more reason to cooperate."

"*Cooperate?*"

"Well, I *told* him you'd never go along with such a scheme. I just knew you better than that. So Damon . . ." She was staring at her lap now. "No, I can't tell you that part."

"Maybe it will be easier telling it to the police."

"No!"

"Where is Damon now?"

"Out of town—on business—but he'll be back in a couple of days. You can't go to the police, Kyle. You wouldn't!"

"Why wouldn't I?"

"Because . . ." Her hand went to her throat in a protective way. Shiny pearl nail polish gleamed softly in the light. Kyle remembered the gesture well. "For my sake . . ."

His eyes remained hard. "I'm waiting to hear the rest, but I'm not waiting patiently. How did you and Damon expect to get the money from me?"

She swallowed. "Blackmail. It was a detailed plan, and Damon is clever. He really is very clever, Kyle . . . ."

He raised his eyebrows in disbelief, and anger heated his insides, but he remained silent, waiting for her to continue.

"Uh...there was the missing plane, you see. They couldn't find a body to prove I was dead. So we knew the insurance company wouldn't just pay up a sum like that; they'd investigate. And they'd probably suspect you had something to do with it, since you were the only beneficiary."

"You knew they'd suspect me of murder."

"Well, we knew they'd have to be sure and they'd probably follow you. Damon knows about things like that. So you can see why we couldn't possibly tell you or contact you, Kyle. They were watching you too closely."

She paused, waiting for him to say something. He didn't. He sat across from her, absolutely motionless, his hand gripping the base of his glass.

"He rigged it all to make it look like you planned to kill me. He even rigged some false...evidence."

"What evidence?"

"A letter I wrote to you that I was divorcing you, postmarked just a couple weeks before I...left. Of course, I intercepted the letter, but we have it. We're keeping it, in case. Also, he has a mechanic lined up who will lie and say you ordered some plane parts from him that could be construed as plane tampering. He'll lie for money—if we ever need to ask him. He did other things...had me tell a couple of people that I suspected you might try to kill me—things like that. All to make you look guilty."

"Yeah, I know about you telling people I might kill you. The detective found that out the first week you were gone. They've suspected me of murder ever since. I never believed you really said it. I thought they'd lied."

"Oh. I did say it. I'm sorry. You see, I had to. If you go to the police now, Damon will produce the letter and hire the mechanic and say he took me away to save me from you."

He grinned bitterly. "Get real, Claire! The police aren't that stupid. What did Damon do with my plane?"

"We sold it in Mexico."

"And you actually thought Damon could present himself to me after seven years, when I would collect your life insurance money, and ask me to give him half, and we'd both be millionaires. Of course, if by some chance I wouldn't go along with it, he'd blackmail me with this stuff you call 'evidence.'" Kyle scratched his head in amazement. "You both must be crazy, Claire, and you must think I'm crazy! This is the most half-witted thing I've ever heard in my life!"

"No, it would have worked! Don't you see? We'd be millionaires! It still can work, Kyle. If no one knows you've found me. We can keep it secret and—"

"It makes no sense," he interrupted. "How can someone in hiding be trying to launch a singing career at the same time? You've got your picture plastered on posters outside this place! Suppose your 'career' took off and you got famous? Huh? I don't get it, Claire. One of us is nuts."

"No one could possibly recognize me. I don't look the same. You know I don't look the same!" She turned her head. "Look, I had plastic surgery on my nose. Remember that bump that used to be there? And on my chin, too. And my hair. I don't look the same at all."

"You look the same to me. Younger, maybe."

"I do? Well, that's different. You…knew me better than anybody else."

"No. I didn't know you at all. Perhaps no better than I know you now."

Her first concern seemed to be the money. She leaned forward. "It could still work, Kyle. We could still pull it off."

"If you think I'd go along with something like that, then you never knew me, either."

Her eyes filled with anger. "We're going to work it together. You said so. You promised!"

"I lied."

"It could *work*."

"It's a scheme concocted by an idiot. What amazes me is that you managed to hide as well as you did. I had a detective looking for you for months."

"You didn't think I was dead?"

"No."

"We were in Mexico for a year. Damon has some connections in Mexico."

Kyle grunted.

She squeezed his hand. "You wouldn't do anything to him, would you, Kyle? I mean, I know you. Damon was terrified of you—that you'd find out about our affair—"

This remark, in the light of everything she'd just told him, amused Kyle. "Are you asking me to protect this guy from myself?"

"Well, actually... his idea was going to get you a lot of money, too—"

"I don't give a damn about that stinking money! I don't want to hear another word about that money, Claire. The whole thing makes me want to vomit!"

At his burst of anger, she sat back, frightened. "What are you going to do?"

"Nothing."

"You won't hurt Damon?"

"Damon can hang himself. He already has."

She turned white. "He'll go to jail! He will, won't he? Oh, Kyle, he'll blame me. He'll say it's all my fault for telling you all this!" Tears welled up in her eyes and rolled down her cheeks, smearing her careful makeup.

"For the love of . . . stop that. Your tears used to work on me, but crying won't work now."

She sniffed and sucked in her breath. "If you help them prosecute us, what will I do? Will I go to jail?"

"I wouldn't know."

"Don't you care?"

He blinked and looked at her steadily, frowning. "Yeah, I care. I think you need help, not jail. Have you been well? Have you had any more of those spells of depression?"

"Sometimes. More often when Damon's gone and I'm alone. I hate to be alone. I think about you when I'm alone and I remember how you used to always take care of me. You used to hold me when I was scared. Damon doesn't do that. He tells me the best thing to do is concentrate on work, on my career, and it does help, but not the same way it did when you held me. Then other times, I'm fine. I'm back to flying again, renewing my commercial license, using my new name. But I think of you sometimes, Kyle, and how we loved each other once. You'd never do anything to hurt me, not even now. I know that."

"You hurt me about as much as anyone can hurt a guy," he said in a flat voice.

"I know. I'm sorry. I know sorry isn't good enough."

He glanced around the room. "You can't be very happy working in a dive like this."

"It's only temporary. Damon says I'm going to be a famous singer someday. Damon says—"

"Damon is finished."

Her eyes grew wide. "Kyle!"

"You're going to get the help you need, Claire, to get back to reality. And you're going to get out of this damn place. If you want to come back to this life someday, then you can—when you're not being influenced by a two-bit crook who has done nothing but use you since he found out about our life insurance. But for now, I'm taking you out of here."

"You have no right to do that!"

"I'm . . . I was your husband, remember?"

She stared. His words shocked her, and he was unsure why. Perhaps it was the finality in his use of the past tense.

Claire began to cry. "You are still my husband, legally. Kyle, I can't stand to be alone. Please don't leave me alone. I need you."

He frowned, trying to decide how much of her extreme mood swings was genuine and how much was acting. Much of it was acting, he knew; he'd seen her performances too many times to forget. Yet she seemed very unstable, and she was completely under the influence of a man who more than likely had a criminal record. Kyle remembered Claire as a competent businesswoman, a good pilot, even a good friend. But there were times—not often, but times—when she had been like a child. The way she was now. She remembered those times; he had tried to help her then.

Had this tendency worsened in the past five years, he wondered, or was she putting on an act? With Claire there was no way of knowing. All he knew for sure was that she was being controlled by this man Damon; Kyle sensed that some of the glitter had gone out of their romance and that by now she was almost afraid of him.

"Forget your next performance, Claire. You're coming out of here with me."

"Damon wouldn't like that. He'll come after me."

"If Damon tries anything more, I'll break his knees." He hated the look of horror that came over her face. "Don't worry, I wouldn't get away with it. The police know I'm here. So does the insurance company. *They* can take turns breaking his knees."

Trembling, she asked, "What's going to happen to me?"

"I'll do what I can to help you."

13

THE RINGING PHONE woke Margie from a restless sleep. It was still dark. The noise caused the sleeping Newton to grunt in protest, and the grunts continued from the living room.

Barely awake, she fumbled for the phone thinking it might be Kyle calling from Florida. "Hello?"

"This is Esther Lee Wurst, Margie. I've just seen the morning paper and I want you to know I'm shocked to think that all these years you've been a respected member of the church auxiliary. A respected member of this community, for that matter. I'm glad your father isn't alive to see the shame of this day."

Blinking, Margie sat up abruptly as the nightmare rushed back. Her first thought was that she'd like to strangle Bill Stoddard. Anger, not shame, engulfed her. Forcing calm into her voice, she answered, "What are you saying exactly, Esther Lee? That you read this morning's paper and now you no longer respect me? It was thoughtful of you to call and tell me that. I'm sorry I haven't time to chat. You just woke me up."

She set the phone back on the receiver and sat staring at the wall while Esther's words echoed in her brain. The phone rang again. She let it ring six or eight times before she finally braced herself and picked it up again. There was the possibility it might be Kyle calling from Florida.

"Yes?"

"My God, Margie!" It was Judy Penney's voice. "What is this in the paper?"

"Bill Stoddard's revenge. I wasn't polite to him yesterday after he wrote the story about Kyle."

"Surely that isn't meant to be a joke! This stuff about you isn't true, is it?"

"Some of it probably is. I haven't seen the story."

"How can you sound so calm?"

"I'm not calm, Judy. I'm angry and stunned."

"So am I! This is libel! You have to sue."

"Even if it's true?"

There was silence on the line. Then Judy's voice came softer. "I don't care if it's true or not. You should sue anyway. Did you have a baby in France?"

"I thought you said you didn't care."

"I do, though. I care about you! Margie, the paper has been out barely half an hour and people are buzzing all over town already. You don't deserve this. I'm coming out there."

"No, I'm coming in. I want to get a paper."

"I'll bring you a paper. But you're not going to like what you see."

"I appreciate your support more than I can say, Judy. But I have to come in. I want to talk to Morgan Smith."

"The publisher? Good! Give him hell!"

"I think maybe I will."

Judy said hesitantly, "It won't be easy being in town today."

"I know. But I have to do it. I may as well face this now as later."

"Is it true that Kyle's gone? Where is he?"

"I'd rather not say. Judy...just how rough do you think this is going to be?"

"Honey, you know this town. Your close friends like me will stick by you no matter what. But the others will wallow in the dirt like pigs. They love the stimulation of gossip this juicy. Some of them will ostracize you. You know that as well as I do. Just try not to let them get to you."

"I'll try."

"Do you want me to meet you in town?"

"I appreciate the offer, but you have to be at work. I'll be okay. I'm not the first person to ever wear a scarlet letter and I won't be the last. I'll get in touch later, Judy. And thanks."

The third telephone call was another hate message from one of her former high-school teachers. Margie hung up quickly and took the phone off the hook while she dressed. Judy was right. This was going to be rough.

THE VERY AIR in the town seemed charged. People stared at her as she walked from her pickup into the newspaper office. Some ignored her; others made a special point of speaking, greeting her self-consciously, as if they were testing to see whether or not she would answer.

She stopped at the front desk. "I want to buy a morning paper."

The girl at the desk didn't know her. She smiled. "The papers are in the rack just outside."

"I want to buy this one from Morgan Smith. Please tell him Margie Donovan wants to buy a morning paper from him personally."

The girl paled and her eyes widened. "He just came in, I think. I'll tell him."

She waited over two minutes, standing at the counter, feeling stares all around her. No one came up to chat. Perhaps they never would again. On the other side of the room, the door to the publisher's office opened, and Morgan Smith stood in the doorway.

"Come in, Margie."

He closed the door behind her. "Sit down."

"I'd rather not sit down. I just wanted you to personally hand me a morning paper. Just to remind you that I'm a human being, Morgan, and I used to be your friend."

"Look, there was nothing personal. The story—"

"My father used to say you were the best publisher this town ever had, and I used to agree with him. I don't anymore." She picked up a paper from his desk. The headlines read, "Rosewood Woman Implicated in Murder Suspect Triangle." "This story is at least half lies. I haven't read it, but I know where Stoddard got it."

"So do I. Margie—"

"I don't have anything more to say, except if this story is as libelous as I think it is, you might find yourself in court. You know what you've done to me—and to Kyle Sanders, Morgan. And you don't have the facts. Bill Stoddard wouldn't know a fact if it stung him on the end of the nose."

Margie turned toward the door, folding the paper. "I'll consider this a gift from you. You've already made more than your twenty cents off me today."

"If you'd just let me tell you—" Smith began.

But Margie would not be humiliated any further by listening to rationalizations on the part of Bill Stoddard's boss. She let herself out and walked briskly through the office, carrying the paper, without looking sideways.

It felt better, she realized as she got back into her truck, to have confronted this catastrophe head-on than to try to shrink from it. Through the years she'd always wondered what she'd do if her secret ever got out. It had been too dark a nightmare to face. She was facing it now, the only way she knew. Her life was her own; no one had a right to judge her! What Margie hadn't expected was the strength her anger gave her, and she began for the first time to understand Kyle's anger.

She had feared his temper, seen how other men feared it. But he had a right to anger and a right to express it; she saw that now. It was part of the force behind his strength. He, too, had been a victim of slander and accusations—for five continuous years—and he hadn't let it defeat him. Neither would she.

Her telephone didn't stop ringing all day. She answered the first few calls. The big question in town, it seemed, was not where Kyle had gone but where her illegitimate child was. Margie refused to reply. Soon she refused to answer the phone at all.

Judy and two other close friends came that evening with the best of intentions, but they couldn't resist asking the questions about her past that plagued them. Margie begged off, saying she couldn't talk about it yet. Later, sometime later.

She needed time to think. The story implied, as Brockmeier had, that the baby she'd given birth to was Kyle's. If she made a strong denial of that, her friends would pressure her for the identity of the father, and Margie was not prepared to divulge it, now or ever. It had been so easy telling Kyle about her past, but that was different; she had been linked to Kyle by suspicion of murder. And she had been linked to Kyle by the bonds of love.

Her thoughts were more of him than of her own dilemma that day. Fear of the unknown kept her taut and nervous. He was with his wife. He had deeply loved Claire once. What feelings did he have for her now, would he have, seeing her again? Would Kyle come back changed? Margie shuddered at the thought that there were no guarantees he'd come back to her at all.

Yes, there were. He'd promised. But he'd promised before he had any idea what situation he was going to confront in Florida.

However grateful she felt for the support of her lifelong friends that evening, Margie couldn't shake off the feeling of being alone. She couldn't really share her heartache with them; they would have no way of understanding what had happened in France so many years ago. Or what she was going through now, wondering about Kyle's reunion with his wife.

The phone continued to ring. She had to take it off the hook in order to sleep that night. And even in the silence, sleep would not come.

In the morning, desperate to hear from Kyle, she replaced the receiver. Within ten minutes the phone rang.

"Margie?" It was his voice. "I've been trying to reach you for hours. All night. Was your phone off the hook or what?"

"Yes . . . Kyle, is everything all right?"

"I'm at the airport."

"In Miami?"

"No, in Rosewood. I tried to call you from Miami before I left and then from Omaha, but I couldn't get through. My plane just landed here."

"You're home! So soon?"

"Yeah, for now, but I have to go back. We need to talk."

"I'll pick you up. It'll take me about thirty-five minutes to get there. Is everything okay, Kyle? You sound funny."

"I'm tired. I hate to get you out so early. . . ."

"It isn't early for me. You know I'm anxious to come."

"Thanks, Margie. I'll be in the coffee shop."

"Did you see your wife?"

"Yeah. I'll tell you about it when you get here."

Margie hung up the phone with her heart fluttering. Kyle was home—to talk, he said. Then was going back . . . to Miami . . . evidently to Claire.

SHE FELT STARES as she walked through the tiny airport lobby. It would be a long time, she knew, and maybe forever before the stares ever stopped.

The second she saw Kyle, Margie knew something was terribly wrong. He rose from the stool in the coffee shop, threw some change on the counter and walked toward her carrying his small suitcase, his jacket thrown over one arm. He looked more grim than she'd ever seen him.

"Kyle, what is it?"

His jaw muscles were stiff, his eyes dull and he was very hurried. No hello for her, just, "Let's go."

He took her arm and led her out of the small airport building into the crisp air, saying nothing. Margie was too frightened to speak, to ask what was the matter with him. Whatever had happened in Miami must have been very bad.

His voice was huskier than usual. "Margie, are you all right?"

"Yes. . . ."

"You're sure?"

She nodded, confused and scared. She was not all right, but it wasn't the time or place to tell him so.

In front of her car, he paused. "Mind if I drive?"

"No, of course not." She handed him the keys and got into the passenger seat while he set his bag in the back.

Kyle opened the driver's door and tossed his jacket onto the seat along with a newspaper. She hadn't seen him carry a paper out; it must have been under his coat.

He got in, slammed the door and slapped his fist into the paper. "The coffee-shop manager took one look at me this morning and handed me a copy of yesterday's paper. Margie, how the hell did this happen?"

So that was it—part of it, at least. He'd seen the paper. She swallowed. "I was in your office getting your mail when Brockmeier phoned there to find out if you were still in Rosewood. He told me on the phone that he'd learned I had a baby in Paris, and the idiot assumed my baby was...was yours. All the time we were talking, Bill Stoddard was in the other room listening on the extension."

"*What?* In my office?"

"He'd come to snoop and found the door unlocked. There was a light on when I came in, but I assumed you'd left it on. I had no idea he was in there."

Kyle swore an oath that made her cheeks color.

"It's done," she said weakly. "Nothing can change it now."

He glanced at her and turned the key in the ignition. His fists were tight on the steering wheel.

"Kyle, please tell me about Florida. What did you find out about your wife's disappearance? Was it as you thought—that she disappeared deliberately?"

"Yeah, with a guy who had worked out a scheme to collect the damned life insurance money."

"How could *he* collect it?"

"It's a long story. A witless plan to blackmail me into giving it to them. It was his idea, not Claire's, to set me up. I don't feel like talking about it right now. I'm tired, really dead tired. And I'm mad as hell. I'm too mad to talk."

Margie watched the landscape from the window—a blur of trees and grass, brown and gray and green—while Kyle drove in silence. She'd been right; it wasn't the same. *He* wasn't the same. He didn't blame Claire for anything, it seemed, except falling in love with another man.

Maybe that affair was over. His anger seemed directed at his wife's lover.

They reached the outskirts of town within five minutes. Kyle turned down Main Street.

"Aren't we going straight home?" she asked.

"Not yet. Not quite yet." His voice was husky and so soft she could barely hear it over the sound of the engine.

Dread descended on her. They were heading in the direction of the newspaper office.

"Kyle..."

"What?"

The fierceness of his voice subdued her, fairly froze her. It was too late to ask why they were here, anyway. He was pulling into a parking space in front of the building.

Two spaces down, Bill Stoddard, on his way to work, had just parked. Margie saw him get out and slam his car door, but he was on the walkway of the office entrance before Kyle spotted him.

"That's Bill Stoddard starting up the steps, isn't it?" he asked her.

"Yes...." She breathed a breath of dread.

He was out of the car before she could say any more. Margie sat forward, leaning on the dash. Her heart had begun to pound.

By the time Stoddard turned and saw him approaching, Kyle was barely fifteen feet away. Fear drained the color from the reporter's face, and in the seconds that it took for the threat to register, Stoddard stood dead still, as if paralyzed. Then he came to life and made a bolt for the door, but it was too late. Kyle caught up with him.

Margie heard the younger man yell a protest. She saw Kyle's arm rise in the air, saw his fist connect with Stoddard's jaw in a blow so fierce it knocked him off his feet.

Margie jerked suddenly to life. She had to stop Kyle from killing him! People were running up from all directions by the time she pushed open the car door. She rushed forward, not knowing what she could do but knowing she had to do something to stop this.

It turned out to be unnecessary for her to do anything. Stoddard didn't get up. He sat on the sidewalk at the bottom of the steps, rubbing his jaw with one hand and trying to shield himself from the attack with the other. Kyle stood over him in silence so deadly that no person in the crowd dared approach him. He ignored the other people completely. When he was satisfied that the reporter intended to remain sprawled on the ground rather than face him, he turned toward Margie.

Her eyes were moist and full of horror. Taking her arm, he guided her a short distance away from Stoddard's horizontal form.

"You're trembling like a willow leaf in the wind, Margie. You've been through hell because of this bastard, and I wasn't here to help you."

"I'm all right," she insisted, aware of a sea of eyes on them, watching their every move. Eyes of people who had read yesterday's paper and believed that Kyle Sanders was the father of her child.

"No, you're not all right. Here . . ." Kyle embraced her tightly. "I haven't even had a chance to say a proper hello to you since I got back."

His warmth was a wall shielding her from pain. It did not shield her from the rumbles of startled voices around them. Kyle leaned down and kissed her lightly on the lips. "If this is what they want to see, then, hell, let them see it."

With an arm around her, he led her back to her car and opened the door for her, ignoring the stares.

"They'll probably call the police," she said.

"Let them." He started the engine and threw the car in reverse.

They were at the end of the street before she asked, "Do you think his jaw is broken?"

"It's possible."

"Did Brockmeier get away from Miami without a broken jaw?"

This made him smile. "Yeah. He left before we had a chance to talk. But I won't let up until I cost him his job unless he apologizes to you, after what happened here because of his damned snooping. If I had the chance right now, I'd flatten his head."

Kyle's rage, Margie realized now, had been directed not so much at his wife's lover, as she'd believed, but at Bill Stoddard for hurting her. He hadn't turned a savage fist on Brockmeier, but he might now—because Brockmeier had hurt *her*.

And she understood the rage. Kyle needed it as an outlet. It was the only way he had known to cope with the frustration, the only way left for him to deal with the pain that had befallen her because of her association with him. If she weren't a woman, Margie thought, she may have found pleasure in decking Stoddard herself. He deserved it, and they both knew he deserved it.

Kyle was a little calmer now. When they were out of town and on the road that led over the hills toward home, Margie asked again about Florida.

"This man . . . talked your wife into staging her own death?"

"Yeah. And they arranged phony evidence to make it look like murder—evidence they were holding in case I resisted going along with it and splitting the insurance with them. It's unbelievable. The guy is a professional crook, and a stupid one. Claire got mixed up with him because she wanted to become a singer, of all the damn things. She was disillusioned with her life, I guess, and with our marriage. This guy really has her under his thumb now."

"Why on earth did you and Claire have so much life insurance?"

"Her idea, because we were both piloting a small plane, and I'd had a close call. Part of her insecurity, I guess. She wanted to be sure she would be well provided for if I crashed. Many people who fly private planes are heavily insured. It's not that unusual."

Kyle was still preoccupied, so much so that she was certain there was something he wasn't telling her. He wasn't even trying to conceal his concern for his wife. Sadness was in his voice when he spoke of Claire.

Carefully, she asked, "What's going to happen now? What's the insurance company going to do?"

"I don't know for sure. All I can hope is that they'll put most of their efforts into nailing Claire's boyfriend and ease up on her. She just . . . she really isn't that well."

"There's something more, isn't there? Something you don't want to tell me?"

"I wish I . . . had better news."

"Does it have to do with us?"

"Well, yeah. . . ."

Her heart sank.

"Margie," he said, "will you give me a little time? It's been such a hell of a few days. The fire and the hospital and Florida and now this damned newspaper. I'm so knotted up I just need to get out and ride. Can we saddle the horses and go up into the hills? I need the fresh air. I want to talk to you, but I need a little time and some open space."

"All right," she said numbly. "If that's what you want to do." *I can wait*, she thought. *I can wait because I don't want to hear what he's going to say.* And the words pounded her head like a pile driver: *he is her husband....*

THE MORNING was fragrant with new grass, the smell of water rushing in the stream and the fine, delicate scent of sun on white sand. Birds were singing songs of summer. From the direction of the pasture came the bawl of new calves.

They rode along the division of their property lines, through a makeshift gate and down across the first hills that rose from the valley to the old dumping meadow.

"Let's not go this way," she said.

"Why not?"

"The dump is over that hill. I used to hate this place when I was a kid. Sometimes they'd dump carcasses of dead animals there." She started to turn back. "I didn't even realize the dump area was on your property until I saw the final papers. Then Ted told me you didn't care...."

"Come on," he said. "I want to see it."

"Kyle..."

He ignored her pleas and continued to ride for the meadow. "Come on...."

Reluctantly, she caught up with him and rode abreast of him over the top of the hill. What she saw before her took her breath away.

Where mummified machine parts and bales of rusted wire had been, where pieces of wagons and bones of dead cattle had lain along the meadow bottom, now there was fresh, new grass greening in sunshine and wildflowers beginning to sprout. The stream trickled clean and clear down along the reeds.

"Kyle! You've cleared the meadow!"

"I cleared it at the first thaw. Nothing new had been dumped on here for a long time. The earth was soft and grass was already sprouting up everywhere. This is the best meadow on my land."

"You're right, it is!" She followed him down the slope to the stream. Insects were humming. Dragonflies darted over the water.

Margie was trying hard to force off the feeling of doom that had overtaken her when Kyle admitted he had bad news—news he was deliberately putting off telling her. News she didn't want him to tell her—ever! She was even more grateful for the miracle of the meadow because it distracted them from what he had to say, even if the distraction was only pretended. She, too, could pretend. Anything to avoid the truth.

"It's beautiful here," she said. "I can't believe this when I think of the abuse this meadow took—all the trash we threw on it."

"The earth turned the trash to compost. Under all the old junk and machinery the soil was getting richer by the year."

"Amazing!" Margie slid from her horse and knelt to pick up a handful of the sandy soil. She let it flow through her fingers. No sign of the awful past was here—only clean, fresh-smelling earth.

Kyle stood over her, observing her. "It's the way things are supposed to be," he said gently. "Yesterday's trash forms the compost for tomorrow's flowers."

She looked up at him as he stood in new, tight jeans beside his horse, holding both horses' reins.

"Are you trying to tell me something? What do you have to tell me that you said is bad news?"

"I didn't say it was bad news. I said I wish it was better."

She stood. He took her hand. "Claire needs help, Margie, and there's no one but me to help her. She needs psychiatric help and a chance for a new start. She isn't well. She's my wife, and I can't just . . . desert her."

Margie felt the pain all the way to her heart. Her worst fears had become reality. She opened her mouth to speak and nothing came.

"I hope you understand."

She nodded numbly and couldn't look at him.

"It comes at a bad time. And losing my house on top of it. All the way back on the plane, I've been going over and over this in my mind. It's just . . . hell, it's not fair to you."

No, it isn't fair! her heart screamed. But her lips could utter nothing. It was all she could do to keep from crying.

He took her in his arms. "Honey, I'll figure something out. It isn't the first time I've had a serious financial setback."

She blinked. "What do you mean?"

"I have to check on the insurance coverage for my house. I don't know exactly how bad off I am there. Maybe—"

"Kyle, what do you mean, financial setback?"

"I just told you. Claire needs my help and I'm afraid it's going to be pretty expensive. She's going to need a good lawyer, too. But of course, in return, she's agreed to give me my freedom immediately without any hassle. That's worth it all and more. It's just that the timing . . ."

Tears sprang to her eyes. She sputtered, "F-financial setback?"

"Margie, it's not *that* bad! I have clients that owe me money and I plan to do a lot of the work on the house myself, and—"

Through her tears, she began to laugh. "Money? That's all? Just money? Kyle, I thought . . ."

"You thought what?"

Wiping away the tears with the back of her hand, she answered, "Nothing. Nothing. Why did you look so sad and upset when you had to tell me this?"

"Well, hell, a guy wants—" He stopped abruptly and took both her hands in his. "When a guy asks the woman he loves to marry him, he wants to offer her the world. He doesn't want to have to give her a house with charred walls and no roof. He'd like to offer her a honeymoon in Europe and—"

"Wait, wait, wait!" Margie choked. "Back up! Repeat slowly and clearly!"

"I said, will you marry me, now that I'm free to ask you? I said—"

"Never mind the rest. I don't care about the rest!"

"You don't? You're sure?"

"Kyle, all I want is you!"

"That, my love, you have."

He wrapped her in the warm fold of his arms and held her against his chest. She could feel the steady beat of his heart next to hers. Here was all the security Margie ever needed—the security of Kyle's strong arms.

"Margie, I love you more than I ever thought I was capable of loving anyone. You've become the whole world to me. I want to make you happy."

"You have. This moment I'm the happiest person on earth. I love you, too. The fear of losing you made me realize how terrible life would be without you."

"Fear of losing me? What do you mean?"

She smiled up at him. "You really don't know, do you?"

"No."

"I'm such a fool," she said to the grass under their feet.

"We'll weather the storm of gossip together, Margie. They think we've loved each other for years and we'll just let them go on believing it."

"Is . . . is that what you think we should do?"

"Yeah. That's the best thing to do. They'll have to accept us as part of this town whether they want to or not, because we're not leaving. Eventually, this will all blow over."

"That's why you kissed me in town today—in public? You were going along with Stoddard's misguided story of our love affair—to protect me."

"Hell, I don't know how much protection it is to be mixed up in a scandal with a guy like me. But better with me than somebody else, since you're going to be *my* wife. Right?"

"Your wife..." she mused, tasting the sweetness of the word on her tongue. "Yes...." She hugged his arm. "We'll rebuild, Kyle! We'll rebuild everything—your house—"

"And our lives," he finished. "Together we can do anything. No one else can touch us or hurt us. Not anymore."

Hand in hand, leading their horses, they walked the fresh meadow in spring sunshine, following the stream that had once tumbled alongside ugly mounds of debris. A yellow butterfly took wing just in front of them. The wet sand of the stream banks glistened in the sun. A bobwhite cooed in the distance, and a hawk, wild and free, circled above them in the sky.

Kyle held her waist tightly as they walked. "I take back that part about not being rich," he said. "I am rich. Everything I'll ever want I've got right now, in my arms."

Temptation™

TEMPTATION WILL BE
EVEN HARDER TO RESIST...

In September, Temptation is presenting a sophisticated new face to the world. A fresh look that truly brings Harlequin's most intimate romances into focus.

What's more, all-time favorite authors Barbara Delinsky, Rita Clay Estrada, Jayne Ann Krentz and Vicki Lewis Thompson will join forces to help us celebrate. The result? A very special quartet of Temptations...

- **Four striking covers**
- **Four stellar authors**
- **Four sensual love stories**
- **Four variations on one spellbinding theme**

All in one great month! Give in to Temptation in September.

TDESIGN-1

ATTRACTIVE, SPACE SAVING BOOK RACK

Display your most prized novels on this handsome and sturdy book rack. The hand-rubbed walnut finish will blend into your library decor with quiet elegance, providing a practical organizer for your favorite hard-or soft-covered books.

Only
$9.95

Approximately
16" x 8"
when assembled

Assembles in seconds!

To order, rush your name, address and zip code, along with a check or money order for $10.70* ($9.95 plus 75¢ postage and handling) payable to *Harlequin Reader Service*:

Harlequin Reader Service
Book Rack Offer
901 Fuhrmann Blvd.
P.O. Box 1396
Buffalo, NY 14269-1396

Offer not available in Canada.

BKR-1A

*New York and Iowa residents add appropriate sales tax.

HARLEQUIN SIGNATURE EDITION

VIOLET WINSPEAR

HOUSE OF STORMS

Editorial secretary Debra Hartway travels to the Salvador family's rugged Cornish island home to work on Jack Salvador's latest book. Disturbing questions hang in the troubled air over Lovelis Island. What or who had caused the tragic death of Jack's young wife? Why did Jack stay away from the home and, more especially, the baby son he loved so well? And—why should Rodare, Jack's brother, who had proved himself a man of the highest integrity, constantly invade Debra's thoughts with such passionate, dark desires...?

Violet Winspear, who has written more than 65 romance novels translated worldwide into 18 languages, is one of Harlequin's best-loved and bestselling authors. HOUSE OF STORMS, her second title in the Harlequin Signature Edition program, is a full-length novel rich in romantic tradition and intriguingly spiced with an atmosphere of danger and mystery.

Watch for HOUSE OF STORMS—coming in October!   HOFS-1